ESCAPE FROM A VIDEO GAME

MYSTERY ON THE STARSHIP CRUSADER

Andrews McMeel Publishing
a division of Andrews McMeel Universal
1130 Walnut Street, Kansas City, Missouri 64106

www.andrewsmcmeel.com

21 22 23 24 25 RR2 10 9 8 7 6 5 4 3 2 1

ISBN Paperback: 978-1-5248-5884-1
ISBN Hardback: 978-1-5248-6803-1

Library of Congress Control Number: 2020950776

Made by:
LSC Communications US, LLC
Address and location of manufacturer:
1009 Sloan Street
Crawfordsville, IN 47933
1st Printing—3/1/21

ATTENTION: SCHOOLS AND BUSINESSES

Andrews McMeel books are available at quantity discounts with bulk purchase
for educational, business, or sales promotional use. For information, please
e-mail the Andrews McMeel Publishing Special Sales Department:
specialsales@amuniversal.com.

MYSTERY ON THE STARSHIP CRUSADER

DUSTIN BRADY

ILLUSTRATIONS BY JESSE BRADY

WITHDRAWN

Andrews McMeel
PUBLISHING®

Other Books
by Dustin Brady

Introduction

Congratulations! You've obtained a rare piece of Bionosoft technology. This may look like an ordinary book, but it's actually a video game that you can play from the inside. Here are some things you should know about it:

1. Bionosoft is not responsible for anything that happens in the game. Do not try to sue them if you get hurt. They've been sued enough, and frankly, they are sick of it.

2. Only turn to pages you're instructed to in boxes that look like this:

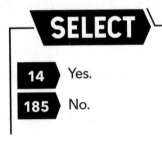

SELECT

14 Yes.

185 No.

If you read the book in order, you'll get confused and leave a bad review.

3. You super-duper do not want to leave a bad review for this book because it's been programmed to emit random unpleasant screeches if it's been rated fewer than five stars.

4. This is a mystery story. Part of the fun is choosing which clues to follow and which to ignore. For that reason, do not go back and try different paths until you've completed the story. If you have trouble solving a puzzle, check the back of the book for hints and solutions. If you run into a dead end, a checkpoint will bring you back to the last save location so you can try again.

RETURN TO CHECKPOINT ON P. 53

5. BOOGERS ARE NOT BOOKMARKS. Goodness gracious, we should not need to say this.

6. Every path in this book has a secret letter that looks like this:

What are the letters for? Can't tell you yet! You'll find out once you beat the game. Don't worry about them until that point.

7. If you run into a blank page, the sensitive electronics might be corrupted with dust. Try opening the book wide, blowing back and forth between the pages, then checking again. If you're confused about the correct blowing technique, please consult an adult who grew up with a Super Nintendo.

8. Select the game difficulty below. If you choose medium or hard, return to this page and cross off a heart every time you run into a dead end. If you cross off all the hearts, you must restart from the beginning of the game.

CHOOSE GAME DIFFICULTY

EASY: INFINITE LIVES

MEDIUM: ♡ ♡ ♡ ♡ ♡ ♡ ♡

HARD: ♡ ♡ ♡

STARSHIP CRUSADER

DOCTOR IZ
Medical Officer

CAPTAIN CARTER
Captain

SSC

ICE MAVERICK
Tactical Expert

STARSHIP CRUSADER

Maddie
?

SSC

CLIVE
Butler Bot 9000

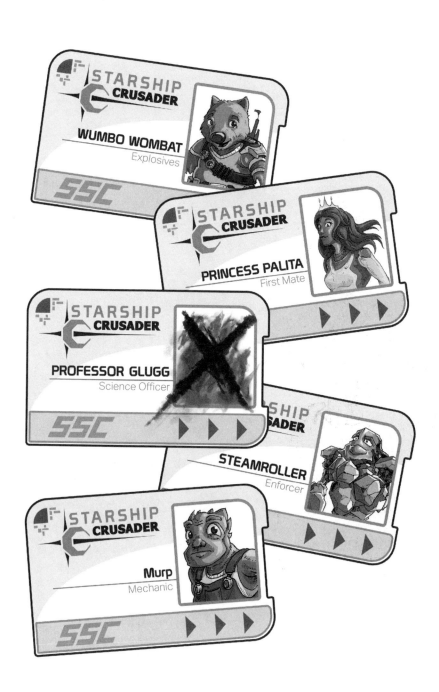

The Adventure Begins

THIS IS A BIG DAY for you. Maybe even a huge day. And while no one would go so far as to call this the biggest day of your life, it's certainly in the conversation for top 20.

You see, today, you got mail.

Crazy, right?! It's not your birthday. You're not old enough to get junk mail. Yet here it is: a little miracle with your name on it. You turn the package over. It's a plain cardboard box, no different from the millions of boxes that get delivered to adults every day, except this one is special because it's yours.

Who could have sent this to you? Your grandma? A long-lost uncle? Maybe a bad guy?

Wait!

Could this be a bomb?!

You hold the package to your ear. It's not ticking. (Do real bombs tick, or is that just a movie thing?) Of course, bad guys don't usually mail explosives to kids, but here you are, holding a package addressed to you even though it's not your birthday, so the rules of everyday life don't exactly apply to today, do they?

You finally work up enough courage to slice open the box. You slowly lift the flaps and wince. Nothing explodes. This is a great sign. You look inside to find . . . this book.

Your heart sinks a little. Books are definitely better than bombs, but nowhere near as cool as any of the possibilities that were going through your head moments ago (video game, block of gold, alien technology, etc.). You open the book and immediately get blinded by a flash of light.

Alien technology! You stumble backward. A hologram of a man pops up. The six-inch little guy is wearing a crisp dress shirt with the top two buttons unbuttoned like he thinks he's James Bond, except he looks way too out of shape to play a Hollywood superspy. He's smiling that smile famous people do when they're surprising fans on TV, which makes you feel a little bad because you don't know who he is.

"Hey," the hologram says.

"Uh, hi."

"I'm James Desmond Pemberton, and I'd like to invite you to play a special game. I can't tell you much about it, but trust me that it will be worth your while. Win, and I'll share a great treasure with you. Lose, and you die."

Your eyes get wide, and you reach to slam the book closed.

"Kidding!" the man says. "Kidding, kidding, kidding. Kind of. It's a video game thing. I wish I could explain more, but this is a recording, and I'm almost out of time. If you're up for the game, simply tap 'YES.' If it's not for you, no biggie. Oh, um, one more thi—"

The hologram cuts off midsentence. It's replaced by two floating buttons—YES and NO. You stare at the buttons, then run to your computer. This day just went from top 20 to top 3.

You look up James Desmond Pemberton. Turns out that he's famous enough to have his own Wikipedia page, but not nearly famous enough to be smiling that smile. He started a tech company with a boring name 10 years ago, then cashed out for a lot of money and hasn't done much since. The only other thing of interest on the page is a picture of Mr. Pemberton in his trimmer days wearing a Sherlock Holmes hat.

Hmm, the Pemberton guy does have a lot of money. But what about the game? You search for "Starship Crusader," and a video game named *Galaxy Chase* pops up. There's not much online about it because it got abandoned pretty early in development. There's some concept art, a fan-made trailer, and . . .

A single word makes you freeze.

Bionosoft.

That's the company that got in trouble for trapping people in video games, isn't it? You realize that this whole thing is very, very real, and you're about to be faced with the biggest choice of your life on the biggest day of your life. Do you want to play Pemberton's game?

SELECT

14 ▶ Yes.

185 ▶ No.

YOU TRY PRESSING the floating "yes" button, but your hand goes through both the button and the book. Now your hand's stuck!

"HELLLLP!"

You try shaking off the book, but instead of loosening its grip, the creepy book swallows more of your arm. It stops for a moment when it gets to your shoulder, then jumps and swallows your head. You fall into darkness.

After tumbling so many times that you no longer know which way is up, you finally hit bottom. Well, you don't necessarily hit anything; you just kind of stop. You try opening your eyes. You can't. You try moving your hand. You can't. It's cold. You're tired. You know that you're probably in trouble, but you can't quite bring yourself to care right now. You're just sleepy. Sooooo sleeeepy.

Time passes. Maybe an hour. Maybe a day. Maybe a whole week. Then, suddenly—*CLICK*—a light turns on. The room gets hot. Your eyes snap open, and your arms begin to work again. You pull a mask off your face and roll over to find that it's attached to a metal canister labeled "HYPERSLEEP." Hypersleep? Does that mean you're on a spaceship? You sit up and look around.

If this is a spaceship, it doesn't look like any you've seen in movies. Sure, the room has white metal walls. You're lying in a cot with one of those thin, reflective space blankets that astronauts use. There are blinky Star Trek gadgets everywhere. But there's garbage everywhere too. Candy bar wrappers, dirty clothes, and half-eaten fruit litter the floor. That doesn't feel futuristic.

HuuhhrrrchKKKK!

You jump when you hear the sound. A lump underneath a space blanket on the cot across the room is snoring like it's choking on a mouse. You slowly stand so you can turn the lights back off and let your roommate sleep in peace. That's when you discover a new emergency: your feet are green.

Are you an alien?! You hold out your arm to get a better look and notice that you're wearing a lab coat. You also notice an ID badge.

You're a lizard? With hair?! You need to find out what's going on. NOW. You tug on the door and find that it's locked, which sends you tearing through the room in search of a key. Instead of a key, you find a note.

> TO ESCAPE THIS ROOM, LOOK IN
> THE CORNER ABOVE THE DRESSER.

Turn the page and follow the clues around the room until you find your path to escape.

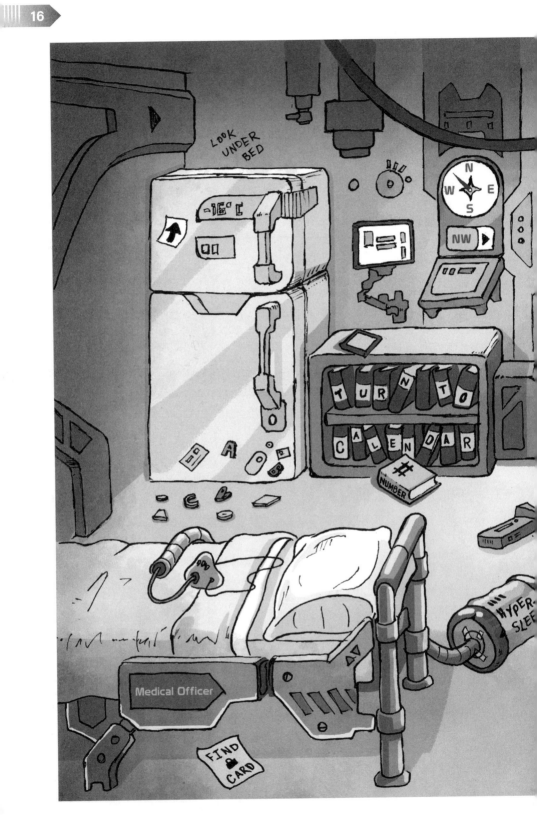

FIXING THE SHIP FEELS like an overwhelming job, but Murp is up to the task. He gets everyone involved and starts making repairs at an incredible speed.

"Wrench," he says with his head underneath the cockpit controls. The princess hands him a wrench. "Light over here." You bring the flashlight around to his left side. Murp points to CLIVE, then points up. CLIVE flips a switch. "Phillips-head." Maddie hands him a flat-head screwdriver. "Maddie!"

"This is a Phillips-head!" Maddie says.

"You know Phillips is the star one!"

"Then call it a star screwdriver!"

"No!"

"Do it!"

"Hand me a star screwdriver," Murp says through clenched teeth.

"There aren't any."

"Then why did you—OW!" Murp bumps his head when he tries getting up. He rubs it while looking through the toolbox.

"I was right, wasn't I? Say it, Matt."

"You have to call me Murp in the game!"

"OK, Burp."

Murp storms off to find the screwdriver. After he leaves, Maddie casts a sideways glance at CLIVE, then changes out of her baggy jumpsuit.

Princess Palita eyes her suspiciously. "Too big?"

"Too hot."

"Why didn't it fit?"

Maddie shifts her eyes. "I'll tell you later," she mumbles. The princess walks toward the uniform. Maddie jumps to block her path. "We need to talk about this later," she hisses. Princess Palita tries pushing past Maddie, but when she does, Maddie grabs the princess's blaster and points it at her. "I said we'll talk about it later."

You aim your own blaster at Maddie. You wouldn't actually shoot her, of course, but you need to stop her from shooting the princess.

"I'm not the one you should shoot," Maddie whispers to you. Then she darts her eyes over to CLIVE.

What do you do?

SELECT

33 Shoot the lights.

30 Shoot CLIVE.

MURP POINTS TO A CRANE swinging a big magnet. "I can hack that electromagnet, but I need a paper clip."

"You're a hacker too?!" you exclaim.

"Not nerd hacking. MacGyver hacking."

You don't know who or what a MacGyver is, but you're excited to find out. You hand Murp a paper clip from your lab coat, then follow him across the room. Murp hides under a control panel, removes some wires, then pokes around with the paper clip. Finally, he's ready for you. "Tap the joystick."

"This one?" You hit something that looks like a joystick.

BRAAANG! BRAAANG! BRAAANG!

An alarm sounds, and lights start flashing. The alien muscle frogs snap to attention. Murp ducks lower and growls, "The other one."

WHIRRRR!

When you nudge the joystick, the electromagnet starts turning, then spinning, then flailing out of control.

"You were only supposed to tap it!" Murp says.

"I did! Your MacGruber thing broke it!"

CLUNK! CLUNK! CLUNK!

The electromagnet starts picking up every metal object that's not nailed down, including barrels of green sludge. The muscle frogs are getting nervous now. You mash buttons until you find one that reverses the electromagnet's polarity.

KABOOM!

Everything that the magnet had picked up suddenly shoots into the room. The sludge barrels explode, blowing a sizable chunk out of the Starship Crusader. That's probably not great for your long-term hopes of escape, but it's the perfect distraction for you to run deeper into the enemy ship. You sprint through the ship's hallways until you bump into another group running in the opposite direction. It's CLIVE and Princess Palita!

TURN TO

P. 82

❶ ACHIEVEMENT UNLOCKED
MACGYVER HACKING

"PRINCESS PALITA!" you say.

Princess Palita turns to you with that death stare that only moms know how to do. "What?" she snaps.

"It's always the person you least suspect, right?" you ask. "This whole time, no one has said a single bad word about the princess."

"She's no fun, and I don't like her," Ice Maverick interjects.

You ignore Ice and continue making your case. "Princess Palita knows everything there is to know about mysteries, so she knows exactly how to stay above suspicion. She's the perfect traitor."

"Let me get this straight," Princess Palita asks. "Your evidence that I'm the traitor is that there's no evidence I'm the traitor. Is that right?"

"I, uh, I guess." When she puts it like that, it does sound a little silly.

"Got it." The princess turns to Wumbo. "What does your little computer say is going to happen now?"

"It says that was a false accusation."

"No kidding."

"And it says we're five seconds away from getting smashed by an asteroid."

"I hate video games."

A ❗ ACHIEVEMENT UNLOCKED
NO EVIDENCE IS THE WORST EVIDENCE

RETURN TO CHECKPOINT ON P. 59

YOU LOOK UP AT THE VENT after reading the last note, then study your lizard hands. Can you really climb up there? You test a finger, and sure enough, it sticks! Awesome! You climb to the vent, unscrew it, and scurry through.

The duct's a tight squeeze and it's a little slimy inside, which you prefer not to think about, but you're able to slither along until it dead-ends into another vent. You kick that vent until it crashes to the ground, then poke out your head. Looks like another bedroom. The ceiling seems to be reflective. Hopefully, your suction cup fingers can still stick to . . .

ZING!

"AHHHH!"

A laser beam ricochets off of the ceiling inches from your face, then you hear a scream below. That startles you so much that you lose your grip and fall. Fortunately, your lizard tail lets you twist midair and land on your feet. You're facing a small, furry creature with a belt of grenades strapped to its chest hopping in pain.

"Stop shooting me!" the creature squeaks.

"I meant to shoot the lizard," a deeper voice says behind you.

You spin around to see a tall astronaut wearing a reflective face mask and head-to-toe white armor. He's got enough weapons strapped to his body to take on an entire alien army by himself. He's currently pointing one of those weapons—a laser pistol—at your chest. You raise your hands. "Is he going to be OK?!"

The astronaut soldier ignores your question and asks one of his own. "Who are you?!"

"Iz!" You motion to your badge. "Dr. Iz! I'm part of the crew!"

"No, you're not. I got in this game a week ago, and I haven't seen you once. You locked us in here, didn't you?"

"I was in hypersleep!"

The soldier takes a menacing step toward you. "Hypersleep? I was never in hypersleep." He looks over your shoulder. "Were you in hypersleep, Wumbo?"

"Can we do something about this foot, please?!" the creature pleads.

The soldier grabs you roughly and rummages through your lab coat until he finds a green vial, then throws it at the creature.

ZING!

The vial heals the little guy with a flash. The soldier shoves his laser pistol in your stomach. "Start talking, Doc."

Your head is spinning. "OK, how did you do that?"

"This is a video game," the soldier replies in a tone that makes you feel like the dumbest person in the world. "I'm pretty sure the doctor's going to be carrying health packs in a video game."

"So this is for sure a video game?" you ask.

"Are you usually a lizard?"

"I'm usually a kid."

"Then, yeah, this is for sure a video game."

"So if this is a game and we're on the same ship, then we're on the same team, right?" You talk slowly to calm this psycho enough that he pulls his weapon out of your stomach. "Why don't we start by introducing ourselves? My name is . . ."

"DON'T say it!" The soldier pushes his weapon deeper into your stomach. "We only use our in-game names! It'll make things easier when we have to start killing each other."

"When we start WHAT?!"

"Nobody's killing anyone," the creature says. He walks between you and the soldier and reaches out his paw. "Wumbo. Wumbo Wombat."

You shake the paw, grateful to meet someone who doesn't want to shoot you. Despite carrying enough explosives to blow up the moon, the cute critter looks like he could pass for one of your sister's stuffed animals. You suddenly realize the inspiration for Wumbo's character design. "Are you supposed to be like Rocket Raccoon?"

"I don't know who that is, but, again, I'm a wombat, not a raccoon."

You've never had a conversation with a wombat before, so there's an awkward silence while you try to think of something to say. "So, um, are you a wombat in real life too?"

"I'm a dentist."

"Oh." You feel dumb. The soldier shakes his head and walks away. You lower your voice. "Who's that?"

Wumbo rolls his eyes. "Ice Maverick. He's telling everyone that he's a big-time gamer in real life."

You make a face. "Do we really have to call him 'Ice Maverick'?"

"Ice is fine," the soldier says. He's pointing his weapon at you again.

"I told you to stop pointing that at people!" Wumbo yells.

Ice Maverick doesn't stop pointing. Instead, he uses his pistol to motion you two onto a cot. "Look what I found." He waves a card in your face.

"Hey!" You check your pockets. Sure enough, it's the key card you'd found in your room earlier. Ice Maverick must have stolen it when he took the health pack from your pocket.

"There's a treasure on this ship, and I'm going to find it. By myself." Ice Maverick backs toward the door with his pistol trained on you. "Don't move. I never miss."

"You literally just missed," Wumbo says.

You start panicking. If you don't do something now, you're going to be locked in a video game with a wombat for the rest of your life. Looks like there are three things within reach that you might be able to use to your advantage. Which do you choose?

SELECT

- **110** Light switch.
- **53** Space blanket.
- **43** Grenade.

YOU NOD TO WUMBO, who then leads the group down the side path. Something about the way he proudly swings his little arms while he walks is very cute. Suddenly, Wumbo stops and turns to Ice Maverick. "You've never won money gaming, have you? You just think you're going to win the million dollars from this game!"

"You're smart for a woodchuck," Ice says.

"I'M A WOMBAT!" Wumbo clenches his fists and tries stomping toward Ice Maverick. Unfortunately, his feet won't move. You quickly discover that you and Wumbo are not only stuck but also sinking.

"QUICKSAND!"

Ice Maverick shakes his head while you and Wumbo struggle. "I told you to let me lead."

"HELP US!"

Ice Maverick waits until your head's almost under the sand to offer his hand. "Maybe this will teach you . . ."

CLOMP!

A giant sand crab leaps out of the sand and teaches Ice Maverick a lesson before the soldier can finish teaching his.

0 ❗ ACHIEVEMENT UNLOCKED
SMART FOR A WOODCHUCK
RETURN TO CHECKPOINT ON P. 76

YOU SPIN AND BLAST CLIVE. Maddie exhales and hands her weapon back to the princess. "I'm not supposed to be here, OK?"

"What does that mean?" Princess Palita asks.

"My brother, Matt, or Burp, or whatever I'm supposed to call him, got this weird book. We watched the hologram guy together, then I told him not to do it. He wouldn't listen. He never listens to me. I tried pulling him away from the book, but I guess I was too late because I got sucked in with him."

"So?"

"So, I'm a mistake! Like, a glitch or something. I don't think the game knows I exist. I'm not part of the crew, CLIVE doesn't talk to me, and I don't have a special power like everyone else." Maddie points to the uniform. "I don't know whose that is, but it's not mine."

Princess Palita unrolls the uniform Maddie had been wearing. She scrunches her face. "Professor Glugg?"

Maddie shrugs. "Who knows! Who knows what's going on with any of this. I'm just trying to keep a low profile so CLIVE doesn't figure out that I'm not supposed to be here." She glances at CLIVE, who's almost finished fixing himself. "I'm scared to see what he'll do if he finds out. Can you guys cover for me?"

Princess Palita looks to you for a decision. "OK, Maddie," you say. "We've got you."

"Thank you."

Just then, CLIVE finishes putting himself back together, and Murp returns with a screwdriver. He shakes it at Maddie. "Phillips-head! Got it?!" Maddie nods with much less spunk than before.

With Maddie and Murp on the same page, your team quickly repairs the bridge, dining hall, and grand atrium. You run into an issue with flooding in something called the "reactor room," but Princess Palita is able to drain it by activating a glowing butterfly with her bracelet. Maddie even impresses her brother by repairing a smashed light switch all by herself.

You finally reach a sign that says "Engine Room" next to a massive door. "Last step," Murp says. "Phillips-head."

Maddie hands him the correct screwdriver. Murp tinkers with a nearby control panel until the door swings open. You groan when you enter the room. An asteroid has ripped through the ceiling and is currently smooshing a very large, very important-looking piece of equipment. You take a deep breath. If anyone can fix this mess, it's Murp.

"Unfixable," Murp says.

Thud. Thud. Thud.

Something else is in the room! Before you can run, a clay giant steps in front of you. "Come," it says.

Princess Palita fires three blasts into the monster's chest. The monster lets her finish, then pulls out a club. "Come now."

CLIVE's eyes light red. "Danger, danger," he says, a little too late. The giant clubs all five of you on the head.

TURN TO

P. 72

A ❶ ACHIEVEMENT UNLOCKED

UNFIXABLE

"I WANT TO STAY HERE and look for clues," you say.

The princess shrugs. "Bucket Brain, can you point us to Glugg's room?"

CLIVE grins and turns toward the ship. Princess Palita and Ice Maverick follow. Murp stares at the spot where Maddie disappeared for a few seconds before storming off to load the power orb into the ship. That leaves you and Wumbo at the crime scene. Wumbo scratches his head, then picks up a rock. "Is this anything?"

You want to laugh at Wumbo for thinking a random rock might be a clue, but you're trying not to be rude, so you take a closer look. When you lean in, you notice that the rock isn't a rock at all—it's burnt metal! And something's carved into it.

"Is that an *N*?" Wumbo asks.

It is an *N*. You don't know what it means, but it definitely seems clue-ish. You pocket the metal and turn to Wumbo. "Let's keep this between us, OK?"

"Hey, ding-dongs!"

You jump when you hear the voice. Ice is shouting at you over the edge of the canyon. "We found something you need to see!"

TURN TO

P.136

R ❗ ACHIEVEMENT UNLOCKED
CLUE-ISH

BLASTING THE LIGHTS should provide enough of a distraction for you to grab Maddie's blaster as long as Princess Palita doesn't do anything dumb. You look over and try to silently communicate to the princess that you're on her side. She definitely doesn't get it. You shoot the lights anyway.

"HEY!" both Princess Palita and Maddie shriek. You spin to grab the blaster out of Maddie's hand but totally whiff and smack Princess Palita in the face with your tail instead. The princess uses your tail to yank you to the ground, then claws for your blaster.

"I'm on your side!" you yell.

The princess either doesn't hear or doesn't believe you. She adds tickling to the mix. When you try protecting yourself from the tickling, you accidentally fire the weapon.

ZAP! BOOM!

Something on the bridge explodes. Suddenly, it feels like the princess weighs 1,000 pounds.

"Critical damage to gravity regulator," CLIVE says.

The princess tries rolling off of you, but she's stuck. "WHY WOULD THEY LEAVE THAT OUT IN THE OPEN?!"

What a poorly designed spaceship.

E ❶ ACHIEVEMENT UNLOCKED
HEAVY STUFF
RETURN TO CHECKPOINT ON P. 18

ICE MAVERICK RAISES his fist in a salute to Steamroller. "You got it, buddy!"

Steamroller returns the salute, roars, then runs around the bridge to pump himself up. Ice nods and crawls away.

"I don't think he's got it," you whisper.

"He's got it so we can get it," Ice Maverick replies.

"Wait, what are we getting?" Princess Palita asks.

"Upgraded weapons at the armory," Ice says.

"I can't do this!" the captain whines. "It's slimy."

"The vents have slime," Maddie says. "Deal with it."

"EWWWW!"

When you reach the armory, Murp directs CLIVE to unscrew the grate. You all drop down and take a moment to appreciate the weapon selection. It seems like every blaster from every space movie you've ever seen is here. It's quite impressive—to everyone, that is, except Ice Maverick.

"Unnnnnnng," Ice groans. "These are laser guns!"

"Duh," Captain Carter scoffs.

Ice turns to the captain, annoyed. "Lasers bounce off these guys. If they worked, do you think we'd be here?!"

DING!

Captain Carter can't be bothered to answer because her glowing rectangle is dinging again. You squint at the rectangle, then whisper to Wumbo, "That's not a real phone, is it?"

"No, but don't mention that to her. For the first few days, all she did was whine that she couldn't bring her phone into the game. I finally gave her a rectangle that dings once in a while. So far, that's been enough to keep her distracted."

THUD! THUD! THUD!

The ground starts shaking. A stampede is approaching. Princess Palita points at CLIVE. "Fix this!" Her butterfly bracelet glows when she yells.

"Your bracelet!" Ice Maverick gets excited. He swings the princess's arm across the room. CLIVE's hand follows the point until it touches a glowing pink butterfly on the wall.

"I don't get it," the princess says.

"The butterfly matches your bracelet," Ice explains. "That bracelet has to be a key that activates anything with that symbol!"

Princess Palita looks skeptical, but she walks across the room and touches the butterfly with her bracelet anyway. When she does, a tiny lightning bolt zaps between the two butterflies, and a secret panel opens to reveal a second armory. This room has bigger blasters and jumpsuits for every member of the crew.

"Real uniforms!" the princess cheers. Then she scowls at CLIVE. "You couldn't have told me about this earlier?!"

"Suit up," Ice says.

Every suit has a crewmember's name on its chest. Yours fits perfectly—it even has a hole for your tail. The crew looks like a real team now. Well, maybe not Maddie. She looks like a kid at one of those sporting events where every fan gets a free men's XL T-shirt.

"I can zip that for you," the princess offers.

"Oh, no, I'm good," Maddie says as she struggles with the uniform. When she pulls it up, you get a peek at her name tag.

It definitely doesn't say "Maddie." You can't tell exactly what it says, but it has a few *G*s in it.

Ice Maverick throws a blaster at your chest. "Plasma cannon. Point and shoot. These are powerful enough to take care of the pirates."

He tosses one to the princess next, but she lets it hit the ground. "I'm not touching that!"

"You're in a video game. If you want to live, you'll listen to me. Point. And. Shoot."

Murp strikes a secret agent pose and points his blaster at Maddie.

"Don't fool around like that!" Maddie says as she bats the gun away. When she does, the blaster goes off, shooting a blue plasma pulse directly into her chest. Maddie screams, but the blast doesn't hurt her. Instead, the plasma bounces off of her suit, then ricochets off of Murp's suit toward the armory door at the same moment a space pirate barges into the room. "ROOOAAAAA—"

ZAP!

The pirate disappears in a blue puff.

"YOU COULD HAVE KILLED ME!" Maddie shouts.

"But I didn't."

"BECAUSE YOU GOT LUCKY!"

"I knew these suits reflect plasma."

"LIAR!" Maddie fires a blast at Murp's stomach.

"Stop fooling arou—AHHHH!" Princess Palita screams when another pirate drops through a ceiling vent behind Ice Maverick.

The pirate swings his sword so fast that Ice has no time to spin and shoot. Instead, the soldier dives forward and fires a blast that bounces off of Princess Palita and evaporates the pirate.

There's no time for celebration. More pirates pour into the room. Through the door. Through the ceiling vents. One even breaks through a wall. Ice Maverick goes into action hero mode, diving all over the room and firing two blasters at once. Wumbo tries running away, but he trips over his own feet. Captain Carter protects her glowing rectangle by diving on top of it. The only one besides Ice Maverick to land even a single shot is Maddie. Everyone else eventually gives up and watches Ice Maverick and Maddie do their thing. Finally, the last pirate disappears in a puff.

That's when you hear a noise down the hall.

Clomp. Clomp. Clomp.

Everyone points their blasters at the door. You do too, until you realize that it's the wrong choice. What do you do?

SELECT

166 Jump in front of the door.

144 Aim at the vent.

MURP AND WUMBO SPLIT OFF, leaving CLIVE to light your way. "OK," Princess Palita says. "Here's what I'm—HEY!" CLIVE wanders off in the middle of her sentence, taking the light with him.

"Stop!" the princess demands. CLIVE doesn't stop. "Stop! I command it!" CLIVE doesn't recognize the command. You hustle to keep pace with CLIVE since you don't want to be stuck in the dark. CLIVE leads you down to a level of the ship you didn't even know existed, while Princess Palita points, whacks, and shouts insults that sound devastating, even though you don't totally understand what they mean.

Finally, CLIVE enters a room that must be Murp's workshop. Tools and disassembled electronics are scattered across every surface. CLIVE's light glints off of something shiny. You tap Princess Palita's shoulder. She sees it too. There on Murp's workbench is a metal rectangle exactly like the one that blew up Captain Carter.

CLIVE finds what he's been searching for and opens a secret panel to reveal a hidden room. "Oh," Princess Palita says, suddenly embarrassed by all the mean things she said. Just as you get comfortable in the room, you hear a *CREEEAAAAK* and feel the ship start to move.

"What was that?" you ask.

CLIVE projects a hologram of the scene outside the ship. The *Starship Crusader* appears to be on a conveyor belt headed toward a trash compactor.

Princess Palita leaps to her feet. "Let's go!" You all sprint to the ship's exit. Princess Palita cracks the door open and peeks outside. "There's a guard!" she whispers.

"Can we take him?"

She shakes her head. "He looks like a bodybuilder frog."

Maybe CLIVE can fight him with his long arms. You're about to suggest that when Princess Palita struts toward the door.

"What are you doing?!" you whisper.

"I have an idea," she replies confidently.

Who should take on the bad guy?

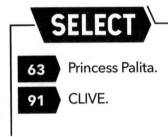

63 Princess Palita.

91 CLIVE.

YOU STUDY THE JUMPSUIT Steamroller had been wearing. From far away, the uniform looks like all the others, but up close, it's much different.

For one thing, the stripes aren't sewn on. They almost appear to be drawn with colored pencil. You pick it up and notice that it's super light. You rub the material between your fingers. While your jumpsuit feels like thick rubber, Steamroller's crinkles like paper. The difference between your uniform and Steamroller's is basically the difference between a NASA spacesuit and a child's Halloween costume.

You're not sure what happened to Steamroller, but this uniform tells you that it was no accident.

> *Now, it's time to investigate what happened to Captain Carter.*
> *Again, choose only one of the options below.*

SELECT

87 Investigate the bomb.

44 Question Wumbo.

100 Question Princess Palita.

"HMM, MAYBE WATER?" you say.

Murp looks skeptical. "You don't sound sure."

"Sounds good to me!" Ice Maverick hastily flips the water switch.

"NO!" Murp reaches to stop Ice, but he's too late.

"It worked, right?"

Your first sign that it maybe did not work comes when the ground starts rumbling. Then, your feet get cold. A puddle forms around your ankles. "Uh, guys?"

WHOOSH!

A river crashes into the hallway. It's a crazy amount of water. Where's it all coming from?

Wumbo answers your question when he waddles past you. "WHAT KIND OF SPACESHIP NEEDS WATERFALLS ANYWAY?!" he screams.

Unfortunately, no one gets to answer Wumbo's question or even let him know that they agree with his stance on unnecessary waterfalls because you all get swept away by the raging river.

E ❶ ACHIEVEMENT UNLOCKED
UNNECESSARY WATERFALL
RETURN TO CHECKPOINT ON P. 53

YOU PAT WUMBO on the back like you're trying to comfort the small creature, then surprise everyone by snatching a grenade from his belt. "WHAT ARE YOU DOING?!" both Wumbo and Ice Maverick shout in unison.

You smirk because you have the upper hand now. "You're not going anywhere with that key card."

Beep.

Uh-oh. You look at your hand. The grenade is flashing red. Did you activate it?

Beep.

Ice Maverick runs to the door and fumbles with the key card. Wumbo climbs over you.

Beep.

"Wait!" You panic. "What do I do?!"

Beep.

"You don't play with grenades inside a spaceship, you dumb toupee lizard!" Ice Maverick yells.

Beep.

Ice opens the door. He and Wumbo stumble out just as the grenade explodes.

P > ❶ ACHIEVEMENT UNLOCKED **DUMB TOUPEE LIZARD**
RETURN TO CHECKPOINT ON P. 23

WUMBO IS USING HIS NOSE to sniff for clues. He looks very silly. "Find anything?" you ask.

Wumbo slumps his little wombat shoulders. "Nope."

You're not sure exactly what to do because you've never interrogated anyone before, so you sit next to Wumbo. "You're the one who gave the bomb to Captain Carter, right?"

Wumbo stiffens. "I didn't know it was a bomb!"

"I know! Just tell me where you got it."

"Yesterday, we were joking at the lunch table—"

"Why do you need a lunch table to eat space food?" you interrupt. "Isn't space food just mush in tubes?"

"No, it's normal food."

"Where does it come from?"

"I don't know. CLIVE makes it. Is this your idea of an interrogation?"

"Sorry, this is my first one."

"Anyway, we were joking that—"

"Who was there?" you interrupt again.

"See, that's a good question. I was sitting with Princess Palita, Maddie, and Murp. Anyway, Captain Carter had been whining about her phone so much that we thought it'd be funny to give her a fake one. You know, like one of those toddler toy phones. When I got back to my room, I saw the glowing rectangle sitting next to my bed. It reminded me of our conversation, so I gave it to the captain as a joke."

"That was the first time you saw the rectangle?"

"Yeah."

You want to continue the interrogation, but you can't think of any more questions. After a few seconds of awkwardness, Wumbo continues sniffing to signal that the interrogation is over.

TURN TO

P. 149

A ❶ ACHIEVEMENT UNLOCKED
FIRST INTERROGATION

NOTHING CATCHES YOUR EYE AT FIRST, but then you spot it: a bottle of soda. Soda bottles burst when they're left in the freezer, don't they? So why is this one still intact inside a freezing cavern? It must have been brought by a member of your crew.

You try running toward the bottle, but the cold makes you feel like you're moving underwater.

"What is it, Doc?" Murp asks.

You point to the soda. "There!"

Murp jumps out of hiding, sprints across the cavern, and throws the bottle at the biggest, spikiest alien of all.

BOOM!

The bottle explodes on impact. "Ni-ni-nice job!" Princess Palita stutters. Then, everything freezes, time rewinds three seconds, and the scene replays, but this time, the bomb blows up Murp. Pause. Rewind. Now, it's back to the original. You look at Wumbo for an explanation.

"The code is f-f-fracturing," he says.

"What?!"

"The hacks are making it unstable. The system is g-g-gli . . . messing up. It's creating false realities."

"What do we do?!"

"False realities. False realities. False realities." Wumbo's stuck in a loop. The rest of your crew starts glitching too.

"Hold on to something real!" you yell.

Everyone huddles, but now their faces are switching back and forth. Can you maintain your grip on reality?

Study the picture of your crew on this page.
Lock it in your memory, then turn the page
and pick out the real version of each crewmember.

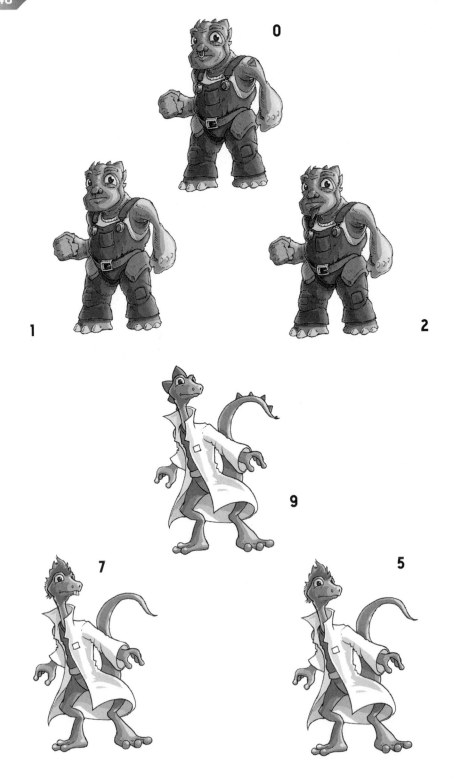

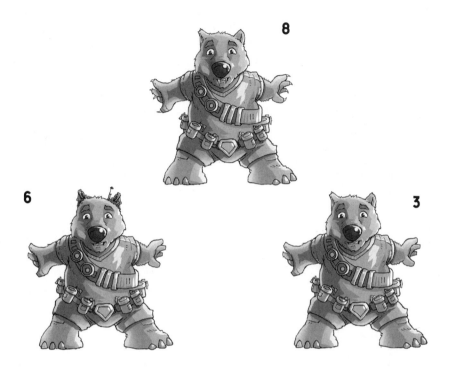

8

6

3

TURN TO P. ___ ___ ___

"SHE'S LYING," you say.

"Excuse me?" Maddie asks.

"You're lying," you repeat with slightly less confidence.

Murp gets in your face. "Maddie's no liar."

The bulky mechanic is an intimidating figure, but you stand your ground anyway. "She's lying about staying where we left her. She had to have gone to the bridge. How else would she have known about Steamroller's y-axis thing?"

Maddie starts to respond, then looks away. Murp shakes his head when he realizes you're right. "Why don't you want to go to the bridge?" he softly asks Maddie.

"Don't worry about it," Maddie mumbles, still avoiding eye contact. "It's this way."

When you reach the bridge vent, Ice Maverick shouts to the rest of the team, "Get up here, now!"

"Nice try, pirate!" Princess Palita screams back.

"Palita, you know our voices," Maddie tries. "We're not pirates."

"THAT'S SOMETHING A PIRATE WOULD SAY!"

Ice Maverick aims his pistol through the vent in frustration, but Murp stops him. The mechanic knocks on the vent. "CLIVE!" When the robot looks up, Murp points at him, points up, then twists his wrist. CLIVE telescopes his arm and unscrews the vent.

"NOOOOOOOOOO!" the princess screams until she sees your faces. "Oh. Hi, guys."

"Told you!" Ice Maverick yells.

Princess Palita and Captain Carter clutch onto CLIVE, who zips them up to rejoin the crew in the vent.

Unfortunately, Steamroller is 800 pounds too heavy to make the trip.

TURN TO

P.34

D ❗ ACHIEVEMENT UNLOCKED
SOMETHING A PIRATE WOULD SAY

"IT'S MURP!" you exclaim.

"No!" Murp yells. "No, no, no! Hologram Guy just said we get to pick the cube person!"

"You don't get to pick anything!" You limp toward Murp and point an accusing finger. "Think of everything the traitor had to set up. Steamroller's fake suit. Captain Carter's phone bomb. Then, there was the stuff that didn't work—the soda bottle bomb and the computer program. Who could have pulled all that off? Not Ice Maverick. He would have shot everyone. Not Wumbo. He's too clumsy. Certainly not the princess. No offense."

"None taken," Princess Palita replies.

"Seriously!" Murp exclaims. "This can't be allowed, right?!"

"I don't care if it's allowed. I agree," Princess Palita says. "I saw the phone bomb on your workbench."

"I don't even have a workbench!" Murp is starting to get agitated.

You go in for the kill. "I have to admit, you threw me off when you got rid of your sister—"

At the mention of his sister, Murp's eyes go all crazy. Uh-oh. Maybe you went too far.

"No offense," you say, trying to backtrack.

Murp takes great offense and launches himself toward you. You both tumble off the arena.

E

❗ ACHIEVEMENT UNLOCKED

NO OFFENSE

RETURN TO CHECKPOINT ON P. 59

YOU HOLD THE SPACE BLANKET like a shield and run toward Ice Maverick.

ZING-ZING-ZING!

All of Ice's lasers bounce off of the blanket's reflective surface. Ice seems surprised, but you're not. You watched the lasers bounce off of the ceiling when you entered the room. You use your tail to wrap up Ice's shooting hand, which gives Wumbo a chance to snatch the laser pistol.

"Can you work with the team for five minutes without trying to shoot someone?!" Wumbo scolds.

Ice folds his arms. "I'm like Batman. I don't need a team."

"FOR THE HUNDREDTH TIME, YOU'RE NOT BATMAN!" Wumbo takes the key card.

Ice Maverick reaches for both the weapon and the card. "I'm going to need those back."

"Too bad, you're in time-out." The little wombat leans on the door and stands on his tiptoes to touch the key card to the reader. The door whooshes open faster than Wumbo expected and sends him tumbling into the hallway chest-first. You wince when the grenades on his belt clank against the floor. Fortunately, nothing explodes.

"He's always tripping, so I replaced the grenades in the front with fakes to make sure he doesn't blow us up," Ice Maverick explains.

"You try walking with these feet!" Wumbo says.

When you enter the hallway, you let out a small "whoa." Now *this* is a spaceship. Everything is smooth and sleek and white without a smudge in sight. It smells like a new car. You pause in front of a window to enjoy your up close view of deep space. A neon green planet zooms by to illustrate how fast you're moving.

"Welcome aboard, Dr. Iz!"

You spin around. It's a robot wearing a tuxedo trying to shake your hand. The robot's face looks surprisingly human with neatly slicked hair and an earnest smile, but its hands are bare steel.

"Uh, thanks," you say as you shake the cold metal.

"My name is CLIVE. That's short for Concierge Lifestyle and In-Voyage Entertainment. I'm a ButlerBot9000, and I'm here to—"

ZING!

A laser flies over CLIVE's shoulder.

You spin around to see Ice on one knee, holding a laser pistol that he'd grabbed from a secret ankle holster. He readjusts his aim.

"Don't!" you yell.

ZING!

He does. The laser blasts a hole straight through CLIVE's chest, freezing him midsentence. "That's for locking us in our room!" Ice taunts.

You stare in shock.

"Relax." Ice reholsters his weapon. "He's an NPC."

"Nonplayable character," Wumbo explains. "He's part of the game. He's supposed to help us, but he's not actually very helpful."

"If he's supposed to help, we probably shouldn't shoot him, right?"

Wumbo shrugs. "He's pretty annoying. Plus, he fixes himself, so it's fine."

"I can't listen to him do the Nalnore speech again," Ice Maverick says.

"What's Nalnore?" you ask.

Ice waits until you enter the grand atrium to answer. The atrium looks like it's trying super hard to win an architecture award for hotel of the future. It's a giant hub filled with spiral staircases, three-story waterfalls, and statues that are supposed to be either aliens or modern art. Its most impressive feature is a massive globe suspended from the ceiling. Looks like an orange fire planet with swirling purple clouds.

"Nalnore," Ice says, pointing to the globe. "That's our final destination. If CLIVE were here, he'd give you a half-hour lecture about it."

Ice leads you into another hallway. You stop at what appears to be a construction zone. There's a panel open in the wall, a vent cracked in the ceiling, and wires, tools, and ladders strewn everywhere. Two crewmembers are standing in front of the panel with their backs turned to you. You're about to introduce yourself when one sticks a screwdriver into the panel and starts screaming like he's been electrocuted. He screams and shakes for 10 seconds before breaking down in laughter.

"STOP!" The other crewmember hits his shoulder. "That's not funny!"

"As long as it keeps tricking you, yeah, it'll be funny."

Wumbo clears his throat. The two crewmembers look at you. Screwdriver guy is a stocky, red alien with a smooshed nose and overalls. His face is covered in grease smudges that may or may not be permanent. The other is . . . a normal girl. No odd skin color, no animal features, no crazy costumes, just an average fifth grader wearing jeans and a T-shirt.

"I'm Murp." The mechanic sticks out his hand.

"Maddie," the girl says.

"Wait, how do you get to be Maddie?!" you ask.

Before Maddie can answer, she spots something over your shoulder and quickly climbs the ladder to hide in the ceiling. You turn around. It's CLIVE.

"Meet our mechanic, Murp!" the robot chirps. "Murp is the man to . . ."

ZING!

Ice Maverick blasts CLIVE again.

"Hey!" Murp yells.

"He locked us in our rooms."

"No, he didn't," Murp replies. "Something broke, so the ship locked down until I can fix it."

"Something broke because you're shoving screwdrivers into everything."

Murp rolls his eyes. "Something broke because this video game thinks I need something to do."

"Then do your thing and fix it."

"I'm trying! But I needed CLIVE to reach something."

"You can't use a ladder?"

"You know how fun it is to make CLIVE do his arm thing."

CLIVE uses a torch to finish fixing the hole in his chest, then blinks a few times and smiles at you. "Murp is the man to call if you ever need—"

Murp interrupts by pointing at CLIVE. That freezes the robot and turns his eyes green. Murp then points to a switch near the ceiling and flicks his wrist, which causes CLIVE's arm to telescope until it's 10 feet long and flip the light switch. Murp grins at Ice Maverick, then turns his attention back to the panel.

"What's the problem?" Ice asks.

"How am I supposed to know?"

"You're the mechanic!"

"I'm 12 years old."

"Oh, come on. It can't be that hard." Ice pushes Murp out of the way. "Just reset all the systems."

"No!" Murp nearly tackles Ice. "If we get this wrong, we could destroy the ship." Murp turns to you and Wumbo. "Either of you notice any clues that might help us figure out what's wrong?"

*Look back at the rooms on pages 16–17
and 26–27. Notice anything weird?*

MAGNETISM

P.111

GRAVITY

P.79

WATER

P.42

YOU SPOT THE TRAITOR to the left, so you dash right.

BLOOP!

The sudden movement must have taken the traitor by surprise, because its shot misses badly. If you keep running right, you'll reach more cover, but that's not going to help right now. Instead, you charge directly into the alien army.

BLOOP! BLOOP! BLOOP!

You twist to dodge one laser, spin to evade another, then fire a burst to clear a path deeper into the army.

BLOOP-BLOOP! BLOOP-BLOOP-BLOOP!

Now that the traitor's attention is focused on you, it sounds like your team is doing its part to thin the alien army. You work toward the traitor's direction, but it's hard to see where you're going with so many aliens around. Suddenly—*BLOOP!*—a laser flies in from your left. That must be the traitor. You turn toward the shot.

BLOOP!

Another near miss.

BLOOP! BLOOP! BLOOP!

With fewer aliens in the way, the traitor is firing more and more shots at you. Still, you press forward.

BLOOP!

Ouch! You were so focused on the traitor that you forgot to watch the other aliens. One of them shoots your shoulder.

BLOOP!

Ah! The traitor hits your leg. The pain is surprisingly intense. You dig deep and keep hobbling. It's hopeless now, of course. You're too slow. The next shot will finish you. But that doesn't mean you can't try.

BLOOP!

The next laser comes, but it doesn't hit you. It hits the traitor. You don't know who shot it, and you don't have time to look. The blob stumbles for a moment. This is your chance! You dive to tackle it. But as soon as you leave your feet, the traitor shoots.

BLOOP!

DING-DING-DING!

For some reason, the traitor doesn't choose to shoot you. Instead, it takes out the final alien, causing the level to blink and ding. The traitor slips through your grasp between blinks. Then, everything goes dark. You wait in silence for so long that you start to suspect you've died.

Click, click. VrrrrOOOOOOM.

It's the sound of a computer rebooting.

"Everyone OK?" Wumbo calls out.

The world slowly returns to normal, revealing that your team is on a round stone arena suspended between orange flames and purple clouds. You try standing but fall back down. Your shoulder and leg are both throbbing.

"What's wrong, Doc?" Wumbo asks.

"I'll tell you what's wrong," Ice Maverick says. "The traitor was blending in with the aliens, trying to pick us all off. I shot him, and he fell right where Doc's lying."

"That wasn't me!" you protest. "I tried tackling the traitor, and . . ."

You trail off midsentence when you realize no one else on your team appears to be hurt. How could that be? What could you possibly say to prove your innocence now?

Before CLIVE handcuffs you again, a hologram appears in the middle of the arena. It's James Desmond Pemberton, and he's grinning like an idiot. "Welcome to Planet Grimwood," Pemberton says. "If you're seeing this message, you've reached the end of the game. I hope you had fun and made some friends."

You wish so much that you could punch him in the face.

"Here's the moment you've all been waiting for." The Pemberton hologram points to the ground, and a floating question mark cube appears. "I hope you've been paying attention. The game was programmed to provide a small clue each time a crewmember died. You should also have noticed some things that seemed off about a member of your team."

You look around. Something's off about almost every member of your team.

"Have you discovered the traitor yet?" Pemberton asks. "At this time, nominate one member of the crew to hold this cube and announce the traitor. If you're right, everyone gets a million dollars. If you're wrong . . ." He grabs his neck and sticks out his tongue. Then, he chuckles. "Kidding, kidding, kidding. You'll just deal with crippling regret for the rest of your life. No biggie."

The hologram disappears, and the team looks at each other. "We all agree it's Doc, right?" Murp says. "Who wants to do the honors?"

You grit your teeth and crawl toward the cube. If you're going down, you at least want to go down on your own terms.

Princess Palita notices first. "Wait! NO!"

Too late. You dive on the question mark cube. Now, the final choice is yours alone.

Who's the traitor?

SELECT

52 Murp.

70 Wumbo.

140 Ice Maverick.

22 Princess Palita.

160 CLIVE.

143 Yourself.

86 Someone not in the arena.

108 The game itself.

PRINCESS PALITA THROWS OPEN the door and sashays down the stairs. What is she doing?! When the guard raises his weapon, she winks and blows a kiss.

Oh no. The princess has chosen a strategy straight out of *Looney Tunes*. She thinks that flirting with the bad guy will make him go "Aahooga!" and forget that he's supposed to shoot her. Unfortunately, that's strictly a cartoon thing. Princess Palita gives the bad guy a bashful wave and says, "Helloooooooo, handsome!"

You've got to act fast. You point at CLIVE, then punch as hard as you can in the direction of the bad guy. CLIVE mimics your movement and knocks out the enemy. Princess Palita looks back in surprise.

"Run!" you yell.

Your group sprints through the megaship's hallways to stay ahead of the bodybuilder frogs. After five minutes of panicked sprinting, you bump into someone else who looks just as scared as you are. It's Murp! And he's got Apple Wumbo in his pocket!

TURN TO

P. 82

E ❗ ACHIEVEMENT UNLOCKED
AAHOOGA

"I'LL DRIVE," Princess Palita says when you hop into the tank.

"Good. I'll shoot," Ice Maverick replies.

You try staying out of the way, which is nearly impossible inside the tiny tank. You finally settle on serving as lookout by sticking your head out of the hatch. The caravan is coming, and it is . . . weird. The giants have assembled an impressive hodge-podge of flame-powered trucks, armored buses, and limousines with rockets strapped to their hoods to escort the power orb to your ship. It's scary, but you take comfort in knowing that the top soldier for the job is on board your tank.

"AHHHHHH!"

You poke your head below to find the top soldier for the job squealing in the corner. Princess Palita is chasing a hairy, softball-sized alien spider. Finally—*SQUISH*—she smashes it on the control panel.

"That's the last one," Palita says. "You can stop squealing now."

"Did you get the nest?" Ice Maverick asks in a shaky voice.

"There's no nest."

"There is! They'll keep coming until you destroy the nest! That's the way video games work!" Ice Maverick's voice gets higher with every sentence.

Princess Palita tries to stifle a laugh.

"The nest has to be somewhere by the weapons," Ice continues. "I can't go over there."

"Don't worry. I'll handle the weapons," Princess Palita says. "You can drive."

"Thanks," Ice Maverick says. "Can you not tell the others? It's embarrassing."

Princess Palita smirks at you when Ice passes her. Even though you smile back, you're on high alert. Maybe Ice Maverick really is scared, but knowing him, he might also be pulling a scheme.

As soon as Ice starts driving, he returns to his old self. "Here they come. You've got a lot of weapons but limited ammunition. Each weapon has its own blast radius and recharge time. You'll need to order your weapons carefully to take out the whole caravan."

Turn the page to find both the caravan and your weapon choices. Only one combination of weapons will take out the whole caravan. That combination's gun numbers will show you where to turn next.

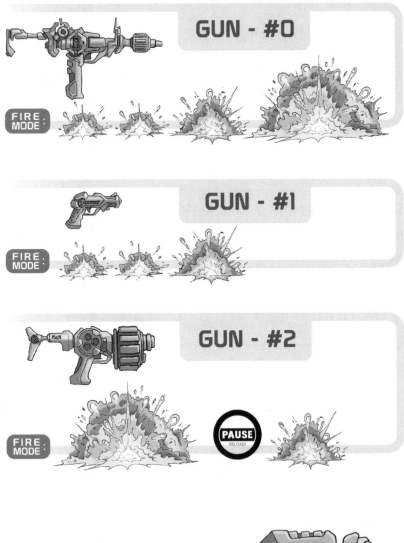

GUN - #0

FIRE MODE:

GUN - #1

FIRE MODE:

GUN - #2

FIRE MODE:

PAUSE
RELOAD!

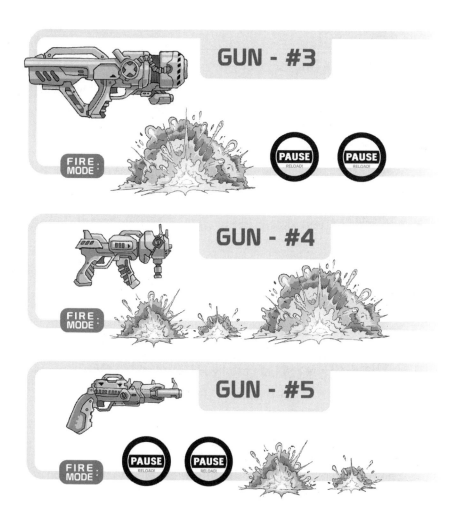

GUN - #3

FIRE MODE:

GUN - #4

FIRE MODE:

GUN - #5

FIRE MODE:

TURN TO P. ___ ___ ___

"DON'T DO IT," you say. "Getting out alive is the most important thing."

Wumbo nods. Just then, one of the muscle frogs barges into the room. Wumbo types something, and the alien vanishes with a *POOF*. Before you can relax, another alien takes his place.

POOF!

Wave after wave of aliens start appearing. Wumbo keeps poofing them, but he doesn't look as confident as he did before.

"Why can't you delete them all like last time?" Princess Palita asks.

"They're being procedurally generated. I can't find the source."

You're sweating buckets, and you can't tell whether it's because you're nervous or hot. After a few hundred aliens, you notice that their movements are becoming jerkier. One appears to have legs where his arms should be. Another twirls in place.

"The code's getting corrupted," Wumbo explains. "The system is overheating."

The room feels like it's boiling now. Suddenly, the bad guys become pixelated. The room turns into cubes. Finally, everyone and everything disappears in a blue flash.

E | ❶ ACHIEVEMENT UNLOCKED
BLUE SCREEN OF DEATH
RETURN TO CHECKPOINT ON P. 82

"ICE, WE ALL KNOW this has to be you," you say.

Ice nods, then marches toward the monster. "Ready to rumble, big boy?"

Urg beats his chest and slowly *thud-thud-thud*s toward Ice Maverick. Ice quick-draws a blaster and fires at the monster. It does no damage. He tries another blaster from his ankle holster. Still nothing. More thudding. Ice reaches down his back and pulls out a long tube. He unzips three pockets, pulls out more tubes, then assembles everything into a bazooka. "Furball!" he yells up to Wumbo. "Toss me a bazooka shell!"

Wumbo squirms an arm out of Urg's grip and produces a bazooka shell that seems much too large for his explosives belt. "Catch!"

Ice Maverick is so focused on his plan that he doesn't consider what a bad idea it is to toss an explosive 200 feet to the ground. The entire crew dives for cover when Wumbo tosses the shell. Ice does not.

BOOM!

RETURN TO CHECKPOINT ON P. 102

"WUMBO WOMBAT." Although you're weak, you're able to muster a cocky TV lawyer tone. "Can you explain again why you told us you were a dentist?"

Wumbo looks annoyed. You put your hands behind your back and start circling Wumbo because you're really getting into this TV lawyer thing. "I think you didn't want us to know about the hacking because you hacked your way into the traitor role."

"That's ridiculous."

"Is it? That's the most fun role in the game. It's what I would pick if I were a hacker." You step closer, ready to twist the knife. "What's the answer key, Wumbo?"

Wumbo looks genuinely confused, which is not the reaction you were expecting. "The what?"

"The, uh, the answer key." Your lawyer routine falters a bit. "Remember? The computer said something about an answer key that you scrolled past real fast."

"Do you know what the computer says right now?" Wumbo asks.

Your heart beats faster. This is the big courtroom reveal. Wumbo turns the screen toward you.

"FALSE ACCUSATION. INITIATE ENDGAME."

ACHIEVEMENT UNLOCKED

PERRY MASON

RETURN TO CHECKPOINT ON P. 59

YOU POINT TO CAPTAIN CARTER. "You're the captain. You should fly."

"Ugh." Captain Carter trudges to the captain's chair and plops down as if each limb weighs 100 pounds.

"You know how to drive, right?" Princess Palita asks.

"Uh, YEAH." Captain Carter grabs the control wheel. "I passed my driving test on the first try." She then accelerates the ship so fast that it causes the princess to mash an imaginary brake pedal. The captain pulls back just in time to avoid an asteroid, then rolls her eyes in the princess's direction.

DING!

The captain lets go of the control wheel to pull out her glowing rectangle. "What is so important on there?!" Princess Palita grabs for the device.

"STOP!" Captain Carter yanks it away.

The princess finally wrestles away the device and squints at it. "Wait, this isn't a phone! It's literally just a glowing rectangle. Why are you so obsessed with it?!"

"WHY ARE YOU SO OBSESSED WITH CONTROLLING MY—"

BOOM!

You crash into the asteroid and explode.

ACHIEVEMENT UNLOCKED
STUDENT DRIVER
RETURN TO CHECKPOINT ON P. 120

YOU AWAKE INSIDE a dim cave with the entire *Starship Crusader* crew. Looks like the other group got captured too. You're all sitting on the floor chained to rusted, broken machines. There's old junk everywhere—not just on the ground but also lining the walls on stone shelves. The clay monster stands in the center of the cave. When it sees that you're all awake, it smiles in a way that makes its face crack a little bit.

"Welcome," the monster says. Nobody replies. The monster scowls and starts pacing. "This planet had two suns. Always. Two suns right number of suns. Then—poof—third sun show up. Arrrrg! Too many suns! Melt everything!"

Your head hurts, and you're having a hard time following what's going on. Is this really part of the game?

"This planet—*ptew*!" The monster spits on the ground. Then, it spreads its arms. "Now, it yours. We trade ship for planet. You get whole planet. Plus all suns. We take ship and party on new planet with two suns. Deal? Deal."

"No deal!" everyone screams.

The monster's eyes narrow. "What you say?" He steps closer to CLIVE, who is actually the only one who didn't say anything. CLIVE smiles back with his dumb CLIVE smile. "THAT WHAT I THOUGHT YOU SAY!" The crazy monster smashes CLIVE's foot.

You gasp. The monster looks satisfied. "That teach everyone important lesson about talking back. Now, I see your ship get boo-boo. Engine no work. That OK. We have power orb on planet to make ship go vroom vroom. I leave to get orb. Fix ship nice. You stay here with Urg. Oh!" The monster raises a finger when he remembers an important detail. "You get Urg in deal too. Too big to fit on ship anyway. Also, he try to eat everything. No good. OK. Bye."

The giant exits the cave through an iron door and slams it behind him. After several locks click into place, it's silent.

You glance at CLIVE. "You OK?" CLIVE remains still. "The monster's gone," you say. "You can fix yourself now." CLIVE glances at his chained hands. The chains must be keeping him from fixing himself. "What do we do now?" you ask Ice Maverick.

Ice sighs. "I don't know."

"You're supposed to know everything about video games!" Princess Palita exclaims.

"Relax!" Ice snaps. "It'll come to me."

You try squirming out of your chains. No luck—the only thing you can move is your tail. You use your tail to dump your pocket's contents, then flick a health pack over to CLIVE.

ZING!

The leg heals with a green flash when the health pack touches it. CLIVE thanks you with one of his classic smiles.

Ice Maverick snaps his fingers. "CLIVE!" Ice points to a spot above Murp's head with his foot. CLIVE telescopes his leg to the spot and pushes a rusty chainsaw down to Murp.

"What is this?" Murp asks.

"Fix it!" Ice Maverick replies.

"I'm tied up!"

"Figure it out! The game has us all in the same room because it wants us to combine our powers to escape. You're the mechanic, so fix it."

Murp grunts and squirms and somehow gets the chainsaw running with two hands tied behind his back.

"Woo!" you cheer.

"Don't 'woo' yet," Murp says. "It's lighting up, but it doesn't want to start."

"What color is the light?" Princess Palita asks.

"Pink."

"Kick it here."

When the chainsaw rolls near the princess, her butterfly bracelet zaps it, and it roars to life.

"Now saw off your chains so you can get the rest of us out!" Ice Maverick yells.

"I'M NOT TOUCHING THAT!"

Ice eventually coaches CLIVE to grab the chainsaw with his feet and free Princess Palita. Five minutes later, everyone else has also been freed. Just one obstacle left: the locked door.

"Too bad we don't have Steamroller," you observe.

"Stand back." Wumbo reaches for a grenade.

"NO!" the group replies. Tossing an explosive in the small cave seems like the worst idea imaginable. However, after a half hour of people pitching even worse ideas, the grenade sounds better and better. The crew finally builds a makeshift bomb shelter out of junk, then Wumbo tosses the explosive.

BOOM!

It works perfectly! When you step into the hot desert, you shield your eyes from all three suns and squint at a distant dust cloud. Looks like it's a caravan of vehicles towing the power orb that the giant mentioned. In front of you are two rusty vehicles: a dune buggy and a tank.

Ice Maverick takes charge. "Woodchuck, use the dune buggy to steal the power orb."

"I can't reach the pedals," Wumbo replies.

"I'll drive," Murp says.

"Nice. I'll use the tank to take out the enemies for you," Ice says.

"No, you don't!" Wumbo yells. He turns to the group. "If we let him in that tank, he's going to blow us all up!"

Princess Palita steps up. "I'll keep him in line."

The crew splits. Ice Maverick and Princess Palita crawl inside the tank, while Wumbo, Murp, Maddie, and CLIVE hop in the dune buggy. Which group do you join?

SELECT

64 Tank.

126 Dune buggy.

ICE MAVERICK LEADS YOU and Wumbo through the ship. When you reach a hallway, flames shoot through cracks in the floor. Ice watches the flames until he figures out the pattern, then picks a safe path. Arcing electrical sparks block the airlock, so Ice bangs on a wall to reveal a secret passage. At the end of the passage is a tangle of wires and glowing symbols. Ice recognizes the mess as a puzzle and solves it in under a minute. A panel slides open just enough for you to shimmy out of the ship and drop to the ground.

Unfortunately, the ship is wedged into the canyon in such a way that the tail is blocking your path. You've got to hike underneath the ship to reach the other side. Ice Maverick puts his hand on his weapon and raises his arm as a signal for you to wait.

"You've played this game before?" you ask.

Ice shakes his head. "But I've played enough video games to know what happens next."

Wumbo rolls his eyes. "OK, smart guy, what happens?"

"You're going to scream."

"That's ridicul—aaaAAAHHHH!" Wumbo screams when a bus-sized crab emerges from the sand.

"Early game jump scare," Ice calmly explains. "Big but harmless." He pulls a grenade out of Wumbo's belt and tosses it at the crab.

BOOM!

Ice pats Wumbo. "Don't worry, little guy. Stay behind me, and you'll be safe." Wumbo looks annoyed both because Ice was right and because he was so cocky about it.

You try to keep Ice talking so you can learn more about him. "You know a lot about video games."

"I should. I'm a professional."

Wumbo scoffs. "Professionals make money from a profession."

"I make money."

"How much?" Wumbo asks.

"A million dollars."

"I don't believe you."

Ice Maverick shrugs and blasts a spiky alien that's mostly fangs.

"What's your name?" Wumbo asks. "I'll look you up."

"Nice try."

"No, seriously. You must be famous if you've made that kind of money from gaming. At least tell me what team you're on."

Ice Maverick kills an enormous scorpion with a no-look shot. "I work alone."

Wumbo scoffs. "Are you trying to talk like you're in an action movie, or do you seriously not realize you're doing it?"

Instead of answering, Ice runs ahead to grab a glowing pickax off the ground before you or Wumbo can.

"What's that?" Wumbo asks.

"Don't worry about it."

"You're not as cool as you think you are."

"I'm not here to make friends."

"STOP TALKING LIKE THAT!"

"No offense, but I've seen it a million times," Ice says. "If you work as a team, you'll eventually have to sacrifice yourself for the team. That's a dumb deal when money's on the line."

You arrive at a section of canyon where boulders have fallen to block your path. The rocks are large but cracked. Wumbo points to a side path. "Over here?"

"Yeah," Ice says. "You lead the way."

Is that a good idea?

SELECT

147 Try to break the boulders.

29 Take the side path.

YOU FLIP THE GRAVITY SWITCH, and your stomach turns upside down. "Did anyone else feel that?"

"Oh, we feel it," Murp replies.

His voice sounds far away. You look up and find him plastered to the ceiling. Before you can ask Murp what's going on, Wumbo floats between you two. A grenade drifts out of his belt. "Don't touch that—it's a real one!" Wumbo says, pointing at the grenade.

"DON'T POINT!" Ice Maverick yells.

Too late. CLIVE's eyes turn green, and his hand starts telescoping. You jump to intercept CLIVE's arm, but gravity chooses that exact moment to act up again, sending you flying straight into the grenade.

F ⓘ ACHIEVEMENT UNLOCKED
IT'S NOT POLITE TO POINT
RETURN TO CHECKPOINT ON P. 53

"DO IT," you say. "Let's get out of here."

Wumbo turns back to the computer and grimaces. "Sorry," he says as he hits ENTER.

BLOOP.

Everything besides the computer disappears. You're in a white room now.

"AHHHHH!" the crew screams.

Wumbo motions for everyone to shush, then points at the wall. There's a loading status bar that says 1%. "It worked. The next section's loading." He studies the computer. "Looks like everyone's still alive. There's me, Doc, the princess . . ." He trails off when he sees the next name and slowly turns.

"Sup," Ice Maverick says.

Princess Palita hugs him. "We thought the spiders got you!"

"Nah."

"Tell us what happened!" Murp says.

Ice shrugs. "Not much to it. I'm good at this game, I guess."

Something's up. The Ice Maverick you know would never pass on a chance to brag. Murp snaps his fingers like he just made a realization. Good. He sees it too. "Wumbo," Murp says. "Everyone still alive is in this room?"

"Looks like it."

"That settles it, then. Professor Glugg is dead." Murp turns to you. "Which means we have our traitor."

You have five seconds to figure out what's going on with Ice Maverick before you're taken prisoner again. What is it?

SELECT

146 That's not really Ice Maverick.

175 Ice Maverick killed the professor.

92 Ice Maverick released the spiders on purpose.

YOU'LL HAVE TO CATCH UP LATER because plodding footsteps are echoing behind you. You sprint around the next corner, then skid to a stop. Your path is blocked by a wall full of cracks. Murp punches the wall, but nothing happens. He slams his shoulder into it. Nothing. He directs CLIVE to punch it. CLIVE breaks his hand.

"We can break through if we all work together!" Princess Palita says.

"We could break through if we still had Steamroller," Murp replies. "Or maybe if Wumbo still had his grenades."

"What do we do?" the princess asks CLIVE as if he's going to suddenly start spouting helpful information this late in the game.

CLIVE remains silent while he repairs his hand, but you happen to spot a skinny door that blends into the wall. "In there!"

The door leads to a server room exactly like the one on board the *Starship Crusader*, except it's smaller and grungier. Everyone gets excited.

"Wumbo!" the princess exclaims. "Do your hacking thingy again!"

"And how do you expect me to type?"

"I'll type for you!"

"OK, type 'run.cpl,' then . . ."

"Wait, wait, wait," the princess interrupts, pecking at the keyboard. "R-u-n. Now, is there a space before 'dot'?"

"No!"

The hallway footsteps are getting closer, and you're getting nervous.

"OK. R-u-n-d-o-t . . ."

"You type a period! Not the word 'dot'!"

"Sheesh, no need to get huffy. R-u-n-period. Uh-oh, I did a comma, not a period. How do I backspace?"

Murp gets so frustrated that he rips two wires from the wall and jams them into Wumbo like snowman arms. "Type!" he yells.

Somehow, Wumbo's able to type better with wires than Princess Palita could with fingers. You'd learned to expect weird from this game, but you couldn't have dreamed that you'd be pinning all your hopes on a hacker apple with wires for arms. You all lean in nervously. "Are you close?" Princess Palita finally asks.

"Almost there," Wumbo says before hitting ENTER. He transforms back into a wombat and grins at your group. "Much better!"

THUD-THUD-THUD-THUD!

The footsteps are right outside your door now.

"You didn't delete the bad guys!" the princess hisses.

"I'm not going to," Wumbo replies.

"WHAT?!"

"Deleting them doesn't solve our problem. We'll just keep running into walls we can't break or enemies we can't fight. We need our whole crew to beat the game the right way. I want to keep going. I really do. But I have to skip to the end of the game or we all die without getting a chance to solve the mystery."

"We don't know who the traitor is yet!" Princess Palita protests.

"Then we'd better start figuring it out." Wumbo types some more, then suddenly stops. His breathing quickens.

"Can you do it?" Murp asks.

"Yeah."

"Then do it!"

"That might not be a good idea." Wumbo takes a deep breath. "I'd have to take the system offline."

"So?!"

"So if someone dies while the system is offline, I don't think they'll make it back to the real world."

"Do it anyway."

"Don't!" Princess Palita argues.

Looks like you're the tie-breaking vote. What do you think?

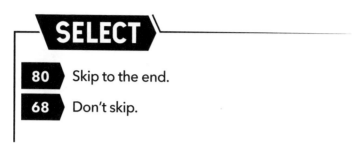

SELECT

80 Skip to the end.

68 Don't skip.

YOU'VE GOT A REVELATION that will blow everyone's minds. You struggle to your feet and confidently state, "The traitor is not here."

"It's a ghost?" Ice Maverick asks, looking like his mind is very much not blown.

"No! Not a ghost! Although the traitor—or traitors—are so good that they may as well be ghosts."

"It's not a ghost. The system says the traitor's here," Wumbo says from behind his computer screen.

"The system is the ghost! It's in on it!"

"Now the system is saying that we'll be smashed by an asteroid in five seconds because we guessed wrong."

"Ha! It's bluffing! Watch. Five, four, three, two, one." You point to the sky, and an asteroid smashes you right on schedule.

T ❗ ACHIEVEMENT UNLOCKED
THE GHOST
RETURN TO CHECKPOINT ON P. 59

YOU NEED TO LEARN MORE about this fake phone that had Captain Carter so infatuated. You spend the next 10 minutes gathering enough pieces off of the ground that you can reassemble most of the rectangle.

When you push the last piece into place, the rectangle sparks. You jump back. Its screen fizzles and putzes, then briefly flashes something. Looks like it could be the letter *C*. This action seems to have sapped the last of the device's energy, because once the letter goes away, you can't get the rectangle to do anything else.

TURN TO

P. 149

D ❗ ACHIEVEMENT UNLOCKED
DYING CLUE

"IT'S STEAMROLLER," you whisper.

"What?" Ice asks.

"Steamroller is supposed to fight this guy. If he were here, sending him into the fight would be a no-brainer."

"Don't know whether you've noticed, but Rockhead's not here anymore."

"No, but I know someone who's just as strong." You look at Maddie.

Ice laughs. "Funny, Doc."

You're not sure whether this is the smartest or craziest idea you've ever had, but you present the case anyway. "Think about it. Maddie activates bombs like the princess. She throws grenades like Wumbo. Earlier, she was shooting like Ice."

"She fixed something on the ship too," Murp realizes.

"We thought that everyone got a special power besides Maddie, but maybe that's wrong. Maybe Maddie got ALL the powers."

"I don't feel strong," Maddie says.

"Try anyway."

Maddie looks at Murp for confirmation. He nods. She takes a deep breath, approaches the great monster, bounces on her toes, and raises her fists in front of her face like a boxer. She's the least intimidating prizefighter of all time, and Urg knows it.

"Urgurgurgurg!"

In the middle of the monster's gurgly laugh, Maddie slugs his big toe. The punch doesn't look any more powerful than you'd expect from a girl Maddie's size, but it devastates Urg.

"OOOOOOOOrrrrrrg!" he jumps and holds his toe.

Maddie punches the other foot with more confidence. Urg crumples and releases Wumbo. Maddie swaggers close to the monster's big face and finishes the job with a massive uppercut. Urg reels back into the canyon wall, then melts.

The group is so stunned at Maddie's first-round knockout that no one can move. Then, you all rush your new hero at once.

If you watch a lot of TV, you might think that group hugs happen all the time. They don't, of course. Real-life group hugs almost never happen because they're so awkward. This doesn't feel awkward, though. It feels right. You've never felt closer to your crew.

That feeling is what's going to make the next seven seconds so devastating.

When you step back from the hug, you notice a metal ball stuck on Maddie's head. It's glowing pink. "DON'T TOUCH THAT!"

"Touch what?" Maddie pats her head, which causes the ball to turn red and start beeping. "Ahhh!" Maddie tears at the ball, but she can't remove the sticky bomb. Everyone dives away right before the explosion.

BOOM!

When you look back, Maddie's gone.

"NO!" Murp cries. "Maddie! MADDIE!"

You know that Maddie's fine. She's back home, safe from monsters, bombs, and traitors. She probably didn't even feel the explosion. None of that makes this easier to stomach.

The princess clenches her jaw. Like the rest of you, she'd gotten swept up in the adventure, but she's back on the case. "Let's find Professor Glugg."

"No!" Murp yells. "We need to find out what happened to Maddie!"

"How do you think we'll do that?" Princess Palita snaps. "The evidence exploded. I didn't see who stuck that bomb on her head. Did you? I don't suppose they have security cameras in a hole that opened 10 minutes ago. So how do you think staying down here is going to help us solve anything?"

Murp stares angrily at the ground.

"We need to learn more about Professor Glugg, and we need to learn it now," the princess continues. "Why hasn't he shown up yet? Is he hiding something? Doc, you said he was sleeping in your room, right? Can you show us where that is?"

SELECT

136 Right this way.

32 You go ahead. I'll stick around.

"CAN I TRY SOMETHING FIRST?" you ask Princess Palita. You open the door a crack, point to CLIVE, then point to the bad guy's shoulder. CLIVE snakes out his arm, taps his shoulder, then quickly pulls back.

You hold your breath when the alien turns around. If this were real life, he'd call for backup right now and have you surrounded. But video games are different. Bad guys in video games must investigate every strange occurrence for themselves, no matter how absurd. The alien slowly walks toward the door.

Your team presses your backs against the wall. As soon as the bad guy steps inside the ship, you point to CLIVE, then slide your foot. CLIVE extends his leg far enough to trip the alien.

"ROWWWRR!"

All three of you run. Your stunt didn't buy a lot of time, but it turns out to be enough since these aliens are super slow. You race through a maze of hallways until you bump into someone else running just as fast as you. It's Murp, and he's got Apple Wumbo in his pocket. "How did you get here?!" you all yell at once.

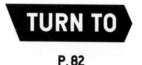

TURN TO

P. 82

❗ ACHIEVEMENT UNLOCKED
DUMB GUARD

YOU TURN TO ICE MAVERICK. "You brought that spider nest onto the ship."

"What are you talking about?" Ice asks in a mocking tone.

"You had a backpack covered in webs while we were fighting that big monster. Now it's gone."

"That's ridiculous."

But Wumbo doesn't think it's ridiculous. "You told me that it'd be stupid to sacrifice yourself for the group."

Ice shrugs. "People change."

"You also told me that you'd never change."

Ice Maverick considers arguing, then shrugs. "Fine, ya got me," he replies casually. "I brought the spiders on board the ship."

Everyone gasps.

"Oh, come on, they can't actually hurt anyone. They just look scary."

"Then why do it?" the princess asks.

"To get away from you guys! This group is like a sinking ship. What happens when you need Steamroller to break something for you? How about when you need information from Professor Glugg? It's impossible to win without the people who've already died. I decided to bail, watch you get killed, then figure out how to win on my own."

"You are truly the worst," Wumbo says.

"Good thing I never change so you already knew that."

DING!

When the loading progress bar reaches 100 percent, Wumbo's computer transforms into a laptop, and the level starts reassembling around you pixel by pixel. Wumbo takes one look at his screen, squeaks, then grabs the computer and runs. "Find cover!"

You're in a frozen cavern, surrounded by spiky ice aliens who are launching an all-out attack. Ice Maverick whips out two blasters while everyone else runs behind a chunk of ice. You'd love to join them, but you're having trouble moving right now. You're a cold-blooded lizard, which means the freezing temperature has you feeling very sleepy. An alien wielding a scary icicle sword tries finishing you off with a flying stab.

ZING!

Ice Maverick takes him out just in time. "Woodchuck!" Ice yells as he turns his attention to another band of charging aliens. "Use your nerd powers to help me!"

Wumbo reopens his laptop, checks the code, then shouts, "There's a bomb!"

"Yeah! A bunch of them! They're called grenades, and they're strapped to your chest! Throw one!"

"No, the computer's saying a bomb's hidden somewhere in this level! The traitor must have smuggled it in!"

"Where?!"

"It doesn't say! We have to find it quick!"

Something in the scene on the following page doesn't make sense. Find the quadrant with the out-of-place item, then turn to that quadrant's page number.

4　　　　**5**　　　　**6**

TURN TO ▶ P. ___ ___

PRINCESS PALITA HAS A BETTER IDEA than returning to your own planet to sleep in your own bed in your own body? You don't think so. You wave goodbye and dive through your portal just as the block you'd been standing on falls into the flames.

As promised, the portal transports you home in an instant. You find yourself still holding this book, but there aren't any holograms, and, more importantly, your hands aren't green. You breathe a sigh of relief. You're back. You're so exhausted from the adventure that you fall asleep.

When you wake up, the whole experience feels so distant that it seems like it might have been a dream. Of course it wasn't. You have this book as proof. But as the days pass, it gets harder and harder to hold on to that reality—especially since you check the mail every day and that million-dollar check never arrives.

You start searching the internet for proof that your experience was real. Nothing comes up for several months. Then, one day, there's a hit on James Desmond Pemberton. A news story says that the reclusive millionaire has gone both insane and bankrupt. Now you're definitely not seeing that money.

You can't stop wondering what would've happened if you'd followed Princess Palita.

R ❗ ACHIEVEMENT UNLOCKED
IT WAS ALL A DREAM
RETURN TO CHECKPOINT ON P. 160

YOU SPRINT DOWN THE HALLWAY with Ice Maverick, Wumbo, and Murp. As he runs, Ice pulls laser guns out of holsters that you didn't even know existed and tosses them to the team. "Stay on my back and follow my lead."

Your group skids into the atrium and ducks behind a statue. That's when the alien pirates arrive.

Your skin crawls when you see them. The pirates have spiky armor and oversized swords, but the scariest thing about them is their skin. They're covered in glistening liquid metal like they've been dipped in chrome. The only thing that's not metal is their eyes. Those glow an eerie red.

Thud. Thud. Thud.

The floor shakes with every step the pirates take. You remind yourself that this is only a video game, but that doesn't make it any less terrifying.

WhooooOOOOMP THUD!

One of the pirates reverses its magnetism and shoots all the way to the ceiling to get a better view of the room. It's going to see you any second! Ice Maverick holds up his hand. He's letting them get a little closer. Three. Two. One.

ZING-ZING-ZING!

All four of you fire at once. Ice Maverick is the only one to land any shots, and that's actually a good thing. The aliens' shiny metal skin reflects the lasers back at your squad.

"OW!"

Murp holds his leg. He's been hit.

"Retreat!" Ice sprints back to the hallway.

You look back at the rest of your team. Murp is hobbling on his bad leg. Wumbo is waddling as fast as he can, but he's not going to make it. You've got to figure out a way to save them!

"Murp! Catch!" You toss the mechanic a health pack. When it hits him, he flashes green and sprints to join Ice Maverick. Wumbo is trickier. He's too slow to outrun the pirates and too heavy to pick up. You notice Murp nearing the panel he'd worked on earlier, which gives you an idea.

"Murp!" you yell. "Reset the ship's magnetism!"

Just as a pirate reaches for Wumbo, Murp flips the ship's magnetic field. The metal-bodied alien stands no chance. An invisible force yanks him backward into the rest of his team. They scatter like bowling pins.

You and Wumbo catch up. "Where now?"

"Up here," a voice calls from the ceiling.

"Maddie!" Murp yells.

You all climb a ladder into the vent, then kick the ladder away. Maddie leads your team through the duct.

"You stayed there the whole time?" Murp asks.

"Of course," Maddie replies testily. "You didn't tell me where you were going."

"You didn't tell me you were diving into a vent for no reason!"

"You know exactly why I dove into that vent!" Maddie says through clenched teeth.

"Can we do this later?" Ice Maverick asks. "We need to upgrade our weapons at the armory."

"Wait!" you say. "Shouldn't we go to the bridge first to warn the others?"

The bridge crew picks that exact moment to perform a barrel roll, sending everyone tumbling around the duct. "We can help them if they don't kill us first," Wumbo complains.

"Steamroller's probably inverting the y-axis again," Maddie quips. She leads you through the dark for a few more minutes, then turns left. You stop.

"Don't we go right for the bridge?" you ask.

"It's left," Maddie says. "One hundred percent."

"She's spent a lot of time up here," Murp says. "I trust her."

Do you trust Maddie?

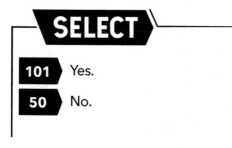

SELECT

101 Yes.

50 No.

PRINCESS PALITA is on her hands and knees, studying something on the ground. "Where have you been?" she snaps before you can ask a question.

You're surprised by the intensity in her voice. "Um, right over there?"

"No, where were you before today? The rest of the crew has been on the ship for a week. Suddenly, you arrive, and bad things start happening."

"I thought you said I was framed!"

"I say a lot of things." Princess Palita replies, slipping into a wisecracking detective voice for some reason. "Now, where were you?"

"Hypersleep!"

The princess narrows her eyes. "Don't make up words around me."

"That's what it's called! You know in space movies, where they hypersleep for years because it takes so long to travel in space? I was the last one on the ship to wake up!"

"I don't know what you're talking about. I was never hyperactive sleeping, and I don't think anyone else was either." The princess smirks like she caught you in a lie. "I'm watching you, lizard."

P. 149

E ❶ ACHIEVEMENT UNLOCKED
HYPERACTIVE SLEEP

MADDIE'S PROBABLY RIGHT—you just got turned around in the dark. You follow her deeper into the ship until she stops at a vent and points. "Here!"

You peer through the vent and frown. "This is the armory, not the bridge."

"Oops. Guess I messed up," Maddie says unconvincingly.

"What are you hiding?" you ask.

"Doesn't matter," Ice Maverick says. "Let's get down there." On the count of three, everyone kicks the vent. It doesn't budge. You try again. Still nothing. Ice grunts. "Must be reinforced to keep people out of the armory. Let's try another one."

Slurk!

You freeze when you hear a sound like goo getting squeezed through a tube.

SLURRRRRRK!

It's getting closer. Suddenly, two glowing red eyes appear. Oh no. The alien pirates can apparently transform into metal goop so they can glop around wherever they please. Gulp.

R | ❶ ACHIEVEMENT UNLOCKED
GOOP, GLOP, GULP
RETURN TO CHECKPOINT ON P. 97

THE SHAKING GETS SO BAD that it knocks over your whole crew. Suddenly, the ground behind you splits in half. The crack grows and grows until it basically turns into the Grand Canyon. Then, from the bottom of the canyon, a great beast rises.

Like the other inhabitants of this planet, this monster looks like it was made out of clay. But, while all those other guys appeared to have been carefully sculpted, this alien looks like someone glopped together a mound of clay and mud, poked eye and mouth holes, then gave up.

"UUUURRRRRRRRRG!" the monster gurgles.

Ice Maverick leaps out of the tank, firing all of his blasters at the monster. They do nothing. Wumbo throws his grenades. Also nothing.

"What is that thing?!" Princess Palita screams.

CLIVE's eyes flash green. "Urg is the protector of Planet Plutron. He weighs 19,852 pounds. In kilograms, that is . . ."

"We don't care!" the princess interrupts. "Tell us how to beat him!"

"Please consult the science officer."

"What science officer?!"

"Please consult the science officer: Professor Glugg."

Oh no. You remember the science officer sign in your bedroom. "I, uh, think he's still sleeping in the ship," you say.

"WHAT?!" everyone screams. Urg chucks another mudball.

"Split up!" Ice Maverick instructs. "Look for a weakness or weapon!" He starts running, and you notice that he's wearing a new backpack. You make a mental note to ask him about it.

Urg grows a fist and pounds his head, causing a mud eruption. You and Wumbo trek back to the overturned power orb truck while dodging projectiles. Wumbo crawls into the truck bed and digs something out. "Check out these grenades!" he yells, holding a silver ball over his head. You help Wumbo dig out two dozen more balls.

"Stop collecting and start throwing!" Ice Maverick yells amid a barrage of mud.

You throw one of the balls as hard as you can. It lands at least a hundred feet short of Urg. Wumbo grabs another ball and winds up. Yeah, right. If you're not strong enough to make the throw, Wumbo's stubby wombat arms aren't going to cut it.

Guess what? You're wrong. Wumbo hits Urg easily. The ball doesn't explode when it hits the monster, but it does start glowing. Although you feel a little bad about not being strong enough for the throw, you remind yourself that Wumbo is the grenade guy, so the game probably gave him extra arm strength. That makes you feel better until Maddie runs over and hits Urg on her first toss.

"Groundhog!" Ice Maverick yells from behind a boulder. "Any day now!"

"I threw them, but they're not doing anything!"

"Did you activate them?!"

"How do I do that?"

"I DON'T KNOW, I'M NOT THE GRENADE GUY!" Ice screams.

"I GOT IT!" Princess Palita shouts. She's pointing excitedly at the monster. "They're glowing pink! They won't explode until I touch them with my bracelet!"

Ice Maverick groans. "Nice going, groundhog!"

"I'M A WOMBAT!"

"CLIVE!" Princess Palita says. She points at the canyon floor, causing CLIVE to extend his arms down hundreds of feet. The princess uses them as a slide. "Wheeeee!"

"Where is she going?!" Wumbo asks.

The princess surprises everyone by having an actual plan. She runs at Urg and holds her bracelet near the lowest ball. When she passes by, it turns from pink to red. The ball blinks for one-two-three seconds, then—

BOOM!

The sticky bomb takes a chunk out of Urg, which seems to tick him off. "URRRRRGGGG!"

He grows even bigger, which means the princess now has to climb to reach the next bomb. Despite Urg's best attempts to brush her off, Princess Palita hoists herself up to the second bomb and swipes that one too. Three seconds later:

BOOM!

Urg starts staggering. Princess Palita continues climbing, which means she can't see what everyone else sees: the giant is about to tip.

"Get down!" Maddie yells. She's too late. Urg topples, burying Princess Palita. "NO!" Maddie zips down the CLIVE slide to help, She has to scramble over Urg to reach Princess Palita.

BOOM!

An explosion rocks the canyon. That's quickly followed by a dozen more.

BOOM-BOOM-BOOM-BOOM!

The string of explosions is catching up to Maddie. You struggle to understand what's happening, but Murp gets it right away. "Mad!" he yells. "You're activating the bombs somehow! We'll help the princess! You take the monster!"

Urg has given up on standing again. Instead, he roams the canyon floor as a mud mound that occasionally belches deadly projectiles. Your group slides down CLIVE while Maddie chases Urg. When the monster finally stops to rest, she climbs him and activates every last bomb.

BOOOOOOOOOOOOOOOOM!

Urg blows into a million chunks. "Enemy defeated," CLIVE says.

The group cheers, and the princess digs herself out of the muck. "What did I miss?"

"UUUURRRRRRRRRG!"

The monster shoots out of the ground with a furious blast. This time, he's twice as big with fully formed eyes, fangs, arms, and hands.

"CLIVE!" you all scream at your unreliable robot friend.

Urg uses his newly formed hands to snatch Wumbo and whisk him into the air. Wumbo shrieks, but Urg doesn't look like he wants to kill the wombat—not yet anyway. Instead, he points to your group, holds up the number one, and makes a "come here" motion.

"He wants to fight one-on-one," Ice Maverick says slowly.

"Who should go?" Murp asks.

Everyone remains silent, quietly hoping for someone else to volunteer. Urg pounds his chest and squeezes Wumbo. "Hurry!" Wumbo squeaks.

Who has the best chance against Urg? Has the game dropped any hints that you've missed?

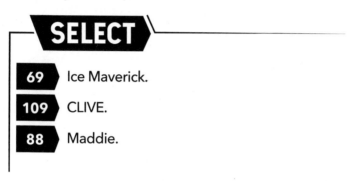

SELECT

69 Ice Maverick.

109 CLIVE.

88 Maddie.

"THE TRAITOR," you pause dramatically, "is the game."

"You're not allowed to do this!" Murp protests. "Somebody take that cube away!"

You clutch the cube tighter. "This is exactly what the game wants! It's trying to get us to turn on each other because it's been against us the whole time!"

"You're saying that CLIVE is in on it?" Ice Maverick asks skeptically.

You glance at CLIVE, who smiles stupidly back at you. That does seem like a stretch. "No," you finally say. "CLIVE is too dumb to be in on it."

"The computer says you're wrong," Wumbo says.

"Ha! See?! That's exactly what I'd expect the game to say!"

"It also says we're getting smashed by an asteroid in five seconds."

"Then, we'll fight back. Together!" You raise your fist and wait for the rest of the group to join you. No one does. Instead, an asteroid lands on your head.

N ❗ ACHIEVEMENT UNLOCKED
THE ASTEROID ALWAYS WINS
RETURN TO CHECKPOINT ON P. 59

"IT'S CLIVE!" you yell. Everyone gives you a weird look, but you continue anyway. "Think about it. This monster wants to fight hand to hand. None of us are tall enough to give him a fair fight."

"He'll break CLIVE in half!" Murp responds.

"Trust me," you say before turning to CLIVE. "You ready to fight?!"

CLIVE grins at you with his same dumb CLIVE grin as always, which frankly does not inspire much confidence. You point at your feet and then to the sky, and CLIVE telescopes his legs super long so he's eye to eye with Urg. Next, you make a fist, point to it, then point at Urg. CLIVE throws a telescoping punch. It does . . . nothing.

Actually, that's not entirely accurate. It presents Urg with something to grab. He reels in CLIVE like a fish. You smile nervously at your team. "CLIVE! Hit him with your left hand!" You swing a fist to demonstrate. Urg grabs that fist too.

Once Urg has both fists, he twists CLIVE into a pretzel. It's important to note that "twist into a pretzel" often simply means "lots of twisting." That's not the case here. Urg literally twists CLIVE into a perfect pretzel shape. It's an unexpected talent. Then, he eats CLIVE whole.

❗ ACHIEVEMENT UNLOCKED
ROBOT PRETZEL
RETURN TO CHECKPOINT ON P. 102

IT IS AN ABSOLUTE SHAME that you've been a lizard for 20 whole minutes without using your tail to do something cool. That ends now. There's a light switch behind you. If you use your tail to flip it off, you can surprise Ice Maverick and steal his laser pistol. You grin a little. This is the first of many tail adventures to come.

Three. Two. One.

CLICK!

You flip the switch without even looking. It's a textbook tail whip that they should teach in new tail school.

One thing that they don't teach in new tail school is checking to see whether your opponent has a headlamp before trying any light-based distractions. Yours, unfortunately, does. As soon as you turn off the room lights, you get blinded by Ice's headlamp, then zapped by his laser pistol.

T ❶ ACHIEVEMENT UNLOCKED
NEW TAIL SCHOOL
RETURN TO CHECKPOINT ON P. 23

"MAGNETISM," you say.

"Are you sure?" Murp asks.

You nod. "I've been in two different rooms, and both had compasses pointing in different directions."

"The ship could have turned," Murp says.

"But there were also refrigerator magnets on the ground and paper clips sticking together. Plus, Ice Maverick has missed two shots, and he said he never misses. I think the magnetism was pulling his metal gun."

"That's it. Definitely it," Ice Maverick says, happy that he can blame his poor aim on something else. When Murp flips the magnetism switch, you hear a pleasant *DING-DING-DING*, and CLIVE's eyes light green.

"All systems back online," CLIVE says.

"If you knew what system was down, you could have told me," Murp grumbles to CLIVE.

Your group navigates a series of hallways until you reach a large cockpit. The cockpit features a huge wraparound windshield with a breathtaking view. It also has rows and rows of screens, levers, and flashing buttons that are almost certainly just for show. In the center of everything is a massive captain's chair with its back to you.

"Welcome to the bridge!" CLIVE says. "This state-of-the-art . . ."

"YOU!" The captain's chair spins around to reveal a character who is either supposed to be a down-on-her-luck beauty pageant contestant or a hobo with a crown. From the neck up, she's a stunning princess wearing a tiara. The rest of her body, however, is wrapped in crinkly, blue tarp. She seems absolutely furious with CLIVE.

"Meet Princess Palita, our beautiful first mate!" CLIVE exclaims.

"You wanna keep telling everyone how beautiful I am, or did you finally get me some clothes?" she asks. CLIVE smiles stupidly, which disgusts the princess even more.

"Ice Maverick gets a full suit of armor, and I get high heels. Does that seem fair to you? Why do video games always do this to girls?!" A pink butterfly bracelet on the princess's wrist sparkles as an exclamation point to her rant. Princess Palita shakes her head and turns to Ice Maverick. "Shoot him."

ZING!

Ice is happy to oblige.

You can't make sense of anything that's happening, so you bend down for an explanation from Wumbo. "In real life, she's a mom who hates video games," he whispers. "She hasn't stopped complaining about her character's outfit since she got here. I think she's wearing the tarp out of protest."

"You've got a problem with my tarp, gopher?!" the princess challenges.

"No! No, no, no. I, uh . . ."

"I HATE YOU!" Another crewmember rescues Wumbo by barging into the bridge. It's a gray-haired woman wearing a highly decorated captain's uniform. She's marching straight toward the princess. "Make him stop! I literally cannot do this anymore!"

Clomp. Clomp. Clomp.

A giant, clumsy monster made of boulders follows behind, mocking the captain with a whiny voice. "Wah! Wah! I'm a little baby who gets my feelings hurt! I'm a tattletale baby! Wahhhhhh!"

The voices clearly do not belong to the characters saying them, and it's freaking you out.

The princess shoves her finger into the monster's chest. "Stop. I'm not telling you again."

"Or what? You're not my mom."

The princess marches the monster to a seat. "Sit there until I tell you to get up."

The captain dramatically collapses into a chair across the room, causing her gray hair to flop out of its bun. "I will literally die if I have to spend one more second here."

"You'll be fine," Princess Palita responds.

The captain sits up. "Oh, really? REALLY?! We just met, like, a week ago, but I'm glad you know everything about me already. I'm glad you're, like, SO into my emotions that you know how much I can take. I'm glad that—"

DING!

The captain stops talking when she hears a notification sound from her pocket. She pulls out a glowing rectangle and makes everyone wait while she taps and scrolls.

"Meet Captain Carter, a retired fighter pilot from Planet Earth. And here's Steamroller, an enforcer from the Gronk galaxy," CLIVE says.

Wumbo leans over and points to Captain Carter, then Steamroller. "Sixteen-year-old girl. Six-year-old boy."

You nod. "Kinda figured."

Steamroller lights up when he sees CLIVE. He points at the robot and sticks his finger up his nose. CLIVE obeys and picks his own nose. Steamroller chuckles, then walks over and smashes CLIVE on the head.

"SIT!" Princess Palita points to the captain's chair. Steamroller walks back as slowly as possible while making fart sounds with his mouth.

Clomp.

Clomp.

Clomp.

"Pbbbthhhhhhhh."

The princess gives your group an exasperated look. "Someone else needs to babysit for a while."

Just then, the ship dips, throwing everyone forward. "STEAMROLLER!" the crew shouts.

Steamroller pulls back on the control stick to level the ship back out. "I was seeing whether the y-axis is inverted."

"Of course it's inverted!" Ice Maverick yells. "You're flying! Why wouldn't it be inverted?!"

"At home, I use controller mods that . . ."

"Stop trying to impress me," Ice interrupts. "I know you play video games, OK?"

"I don't just play video games. I'm GOOD at video games. Like, really good."

"Uh, guys?" Murp says, staring out the window. Your heart sinks. It's an asteroid field, and it's approaching fast.

"STEAMROLLER!" everyone shouts again.

"I didn't do anything!"

Ice Maverick pushes Steamroller out of the way and grabs the controls. When he does, a warning flashes across the control panel. "It's OK, I've got this," Ice says. The lights on the bridge all turn blood red, signaling that Ice, perhaps, does not have it.

"Captain!" the princess yells. "You've got to steer!"

The captain wrinkles her nose. "Yeah, right. That's not my job."

"THAT'S EXACTLY YOUR JOB!"

". . . The pirates," a voice says behind you.

You turn to see that CLIVE has finished reassembling himself. "What did you say?"

CLIVE grins blankly at you until Murp yells, "Repeat! Repeat!"

CLIVE clears his throat. "A breach has been registered at airlock number four. Space pirates from Planet Carrideppo are boarding the ship. Would you like to engage the intruders?"

"YES!" Murp says.

"To engage the space pirates, please consult your science—"

SMASH!

"STEAMROLLER!"

"He let them in!" the rock monster replies. "Someone needed to teach him a lesson."

"He didn't let them in, you idiot!" Murp yells. "He was going to tell us how to beat them!"

You locate a screen showing security camera feeds and watch helplessly as scary aliens with eye patches pour into a hallway. Ice Maverick takes charge. "Bridge crew, get us past those asteroids. Wumbo and Murp, help me take out these aliens. Doc, you can either help the bridge or join us."

SELECT

120 Help the bridge.

97 Fight pirates.

YOU HOLD UP A FINGER like you're going to make a speech, then spin and run. The ship's lights immediately start flashing red. When you round a corner, a wall lowers from the ceiling. Yikes! They're trying to box you in. You sprint faster, then dive at the last second. You make it.

Safe from the others for at least a moment, you try to catch your breath. That's when a black tube emerges from the wall and starts making a vacuum cleaner sound. Hmm, this doesn't seem good.

You stand and immediately start sliding toward the tube. You use your lizard fingers to hold on to the wall, but your tail gets stuck in the tube. It's so sucky! Soon, your whole body gets sucked into the tube, then spit into a glass cube barely tall enough to stand inside.

"This is jail," Princess Palita says when you land. She's surrounded by the rest of the crew, who all look extremely disappointed in you. "This is your home until we get out of the game. Traitor."

R **❶ ACHIEVEMENT UNLOCKED**
SO SUCKY
RETURN TO CHECKPOINT ON P. 136

NOW'S YOUR CHANCE to shift the pressure onto someone else. "What haven't you been telling us?" you demand.

Wumbo takes a deep breath. "OK, I'm not a dentist."

"No kidding," the princess says.

"But I'm not evil either! I'm a developer who makes boring apps for boring companies. Like, digital catalogs for farm equipment companies. Stuff like that."

"Then why say you're a dentist?"

Wumbo sighs. He's clearly trying to decide how much to tell you. "Because I do some, um, hacking on the side."

Princess Palita gasps like Wumbo just admitted to being an assassin.

"Relax," Wumbo says. "It's not like hacking in the movies. I heard a rumor about this game, then I figured out a way to, like, hack my way in. That's it, OK? I just didn't want anyone to know."

"Well, now we know," Princess Palita says. "So tell us what else you can hack."

TURN TO

P. 121

R ❗ ACHIEVEMENT UNLOCKED

NOT A DENTIST

WHEN ICE MAVERICK'S group leaves, you turn to inspire your crew. Captain Carter is already staring at the glowing rectangle, Steamroller is wiggling his hips to a beat that exists only in his head, and Princess Palita is adjusting her makeshift tarp dress. You clear your throat. "Um, what do you guys think about getting us past these asteroids?"

"I've got it," Steamroller says, dancing to the captain's chair.

"No, you don't!" The princess grabs Captain Carter's arm. "Do your job."

"You're not my mom!" both Steamroller and Captain Carter yell at the same time.

"Then, I'll do it!" Princess Palita harumphs and turns to the controls. "Now, let's see—steering wheel, steering wheel, where did they put the steering wheel?"

When the princess's back is turned, Steamroller tries putting his oversized finger into Captain Carter's ear.

"Quit it!" the captain yells.

"You quit."

"So help me, I will turn this ship around!" the princess says.

"HE STARTED IT!"

You look to CLIVE for help. He's staring ahead stupidly. Looks like it's up to you to pick a pilot.

SELECT

125 Princess.

141 Steamroller.

71 Captain.

"I DON'T KNOW what else it'll let me change," Wumbo says. "Give me a second to look through the computer."

You all lean over Wumbo's shoulder as his paws fly over the keyboard. A menu appears on the screen, and Wumbo tabs through it. You don't understand most of the categories, but you notice one that looks promising: answer key.

"That one!" you yell. "Maybe it'll tell us who the traitor is."

"Sorry, it's locked," Wumbo says without stopping.

Murp looks at Wumbo skeptically. "You didn't even try it." When Wumbo ignores him, Murp leans closer. "Scared of what we'll find in there, traitor? Fine, I'll try."

"No!" Wumbo spreads his arms over the keyboard. "If you do something wrong and break the game, we'll be trapped forever! Trust me, OK?"

Murp backs off and glares. Wumbo scrolls more, then leans back. "This one."

"History log?" Princess Palita asks. "How's that going to help?"

"This terminal shouldn't have been unlocked," Wumbo replies. "That tells me someone's already been here. The history log probably won't give us their name, but it'll tell us what they were doing." The little wombat rubs his paws together, then hits ENTER. He reads for a bit, then scrunches his face. "It's an executable file."

Princess Palita looks exasperated. "Stop talking in nerd language!"

"An executable file runs a program. This one is called spritexfer.exe."

"What does it do?"

"The only way we find out is by running it." Wumbo takes a deep breath, then hits ENTER again. Nothing happens for a few seconds. Then the world flickers and Wumbo disappears.

"Wumbo?" Murp calls. "Wumbo?!"

The princess bends over the computer. "Where's the UNDO button?!"

"Don't touch that!" a squeaky voice says behind you. You all turn. The only thing back there is the apple sitting on the office chair. "I'm fine," the apple says, using the part that's been bitten as a mouth.

"W-Wumbo?" you ask the apple.

The apple hops off the chair, which startles Murp so much that he trips backward. "It was a trap," Apple Wumbo says. "I should have known."

Princess Palita puts her head in her hands. "I hate video games. I hate them, I hate them, I hate them."

Your head is spinning. "What's going on?!"

"The program is designed to transform a character into an object in the room," Wumbo explains like this is a normal thing. "The traitor left an apple on the desk, so now I'm an apple."

Suddenly, the lights that had been flickering on the wall start pulsing as one. The ship makes a *WUUUUUuuuuummmmm* sound. Princess Palita throws up her arms. "NOW WHAT?!"

Murp looks at the computer terminal. "It says something about an electromagnetic pulse."

"EMP attack imminent," CLIVE says.

WumwumwumwumWUMWUMWUM—POP!

Everything gets super bright, then it all goes dark at once. You start floating. For the first time all game, you truly feel like you're in outer space. "Emergency lighting activated," CLIVE says as a flashlight on top of his head clicks on.

"Can someone explain what just happened?" the princess asks.

"An EMP attack uses an electromagnetic pulse to disable electronics," Wumbo explains. "That's our lighting, gravity system, and basically everything on our ship."

Obviously, you have a lot of questions, but it's hard to concentrate on anything besides the fact that an apple is talking to you. Fortunately, Murp has no problem talking to an apple. "Who attacked us?!"

The top of the apple bobs up and down, which is probably Wumbo's way of shrugging. Princess Palita floats across the room, opens the door, then leads your group down the hall. While everyone else floats gracefully, you keep bumping your head since your hands are still cuffed. "Could someone get these off of me?" you ask.

It's silent. No one wants to make the decision. Finally, Wumbo says, "As long as you don't eat me."

"Deal."

CLIVE removes your handcuffs just as your group arrives at floor-to-ceiling windows. You squeeze in for a better look. Oh no. A spaceship the size of a small moon has the *Starship Crusader* trapped in some sort of tractor beam. The front of the megaship opens like a giant mouth, and the beam starts reeling you in.

Princess Palita turns to everyone else. "I just want you all to know this is the worst day of my life."

"Try being an apple," Wumbo replies.

When you near the megaship, its gravity takes over, and you drop to the ground. "Let's get out of here," Wumbo says.

"And do what?" Princess Palita asks. "Ice Maverick's not here to fight them. We need to hide."

"I agree with Wumbo," Murp says. "We're dead if we stay."

"Fine. You two go," Princess Palita says. "I'm staying put."

What do you do?

SELECT

138 Escape.

39 Hide.

"YOU WORRY ABOUT STEERING. I'll watch the kids," you tell Princess Palita.

"Did you call us kids?" The 60-year-old captain looks at you with disgust.

"No lizard is gonna tell me what to do!" Steamroller yells. "Especially a lizard with HAIR."

"What does my hair have to do with anything?!"

"It looks like a poop emoji," Steamroller states matter-of-factly before mussing your hair.

"Hey!" Even though you know you're supposed to be the mature one, rage starts boiling inside. Steamroller has a special talent for getting under people's skin. The rock monster reaches down to tousle your hair again, but you spin and whip your tail at him first. The tail whip misses Steamroller but knocks Captain Carter's rectangle out of her hand.

"Hey!" Captain Carter yells.

"HEY!" Princess Palita turns around again. "Do NOT make me come back there! If I have to get out of this seat, you WILL regret it!"

BOOM!

The ship crashes into an asteroid while the princess lectures you. You all regret it.

B **❗ ACHIEVEMENT UNLOCKED**
POOPY HAIR

RETURN TO CHECKPOINT ON P. 120

MURP JUMPS INTO the driver's seat, and Maddie calls shotgun. You, Wumbo, and CLIVE squeeze into the back. The dune buggy starts with a scary burp and rattles like it could fall apart at any second, but it accelerates quickly when Murp hits the gas.

As you approach the caravan, you realize that the aliens have put everything they have into protecting the power orb. They're not only driving a fleet of armored vehicles but also keeping all their scariest warriors in the power orb truck. You could really use Ice Maverick's artillery right now. Wumbo's got a few grenades, but there's a better chance of him blowing himself up than taking out all the bad guys.

"What's the plan?" you ask Murp.

Murp doesn't answer because he's not paying attention to you. He's not paying attention to the road either. He seems to be distracted by all the rusty junk littering the ground.

"Hey!" Maddie yells. "Snap out of it!"

"You drive," Murp says.

"I can't reach the pedals!"

Murp swipes a spring off the ground, then twists it onto the gas pedal to give Maddie a place to put her foot. "Now drive."

When Maddie takes the wheel, Murp climbs into the backseat. "Doc, you've got sticky lizard fingers, right?"

"Sure. Why?"

"I can build something that will help us grab that power cell, but I need your help."

"What is it?" Maddie asks skeptically from the front seat.

"Don't worry about it."

"Matt!" she demands.

"It's a Slug-o-Matic."

"Maaaaatt," Maddie complains.

"Call me Murp in the game!" Murp uses a rock to etch an outline into the dune buggy's metal trunk. The vehicle never stops bumping and shaking, but the outline is surprisingly clear. He turns to you when he finishes. "I need parts that look exactly like this. Can you grab them for me?"

Find the parts on the next two pages that fit Murp's outline below. Piecing the correct parts together will reveal the page you need to turn to.

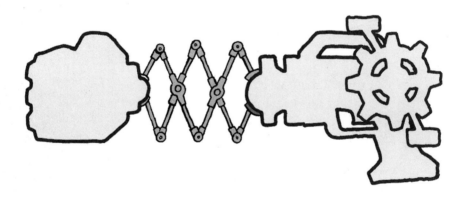

2

1

5

3

4

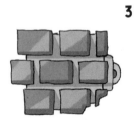

8

7

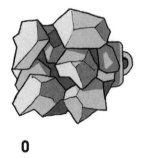

0

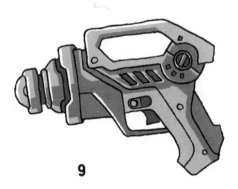

9

TURN TO P. _____   _____   _____

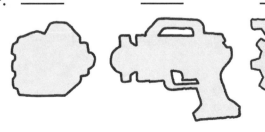

AS CLIVE WALKS YOU DOWN the hallway, you feel the ship sputter and lift off. Murp must have gotten the power orb working. You close your eyes and think. What are you missing?

Automatic doors whoosh open ahead. "Spiders!" Murp yells. You open your eyes to see the mechanic running toward you in a dead sprint. "SPIIIIIIDEEEEEEERS!" he screams again as he passes you.

The automatic doors whoosh open again to reveal the source of Murp's terror: a flood of spiders crawling on every inch of the floor, walls, and ceiling. These aren't ordinary house spiders. They're not even ordinary tarantulas. They're hideous, rodent-sized creatures that could only come from deep space or Australia, and they look absolutely livid.

Everyone tries to catch up with Murp. You glance back and see the spiders gaining fast. Ice Maverick points to a door at the end of the hallway. "Lock yourselves in there! I'll cover you!" Then he spins, whips out two blasters, and takes on the spiders.

Zingzingzingzingzing!

Ice's blasters are no match for the spider army. They engulf Ice Maverick just as the rest of your group reaches the room.

"Should we go back for him?" Wumbo asks after slamming the door.

Before anyone can answer, you hear the tinking of a million spider legs trying to kick down the door. One of the spiders flattens itself enough to squeeze into the room. Princess Palita stomps on it, then slumps. "I can't believe Ice did that for us."

"I can't either," Wumbo says. "He never cared about anyone but himself."

"He did something I didn't understand with the spiders back in the tank too," Princess Palita says.

"Wait, you've seen these before?" Murp asks. "What do you know about them?"

Palita thinks for a moment, then her eyes get wide. "Ice mentioned a nest! He said the spiders will keep coming until we destroy the nest."

"And how do you suggest we do that?"

Everyone looks for an escape. There's not much to work with. You're in a closet that seems to house the ship's computer system. The walls are all black and blinky like you're inside the computer itself. There's a keyboard and screen with scrolling computer code at one end of the room, a half-eaten apple sitting on an office chair at the other end, and that's pretty much it.

"T-minus five minutes to spider containment breach," CLIVE says, breaking the silence.

"What about a vent?" the princess asks. "Can we crawl through a vent?"

Murp gets CLIVE to hoist him up to the ceiling. "Yes!" he reports excitedly. Then he presses his ear to the vent. "Wait, no. I hear them up here too."

"AHHHH!" the group screams.

"T-minus four minutes to containment breach," CLIVE adds.

"Why is Doc handcuffed?" Murp asks when he notices your hands.

"We think he's the traitor," Princess Palita replies.

Suddenly, Murp's whole demeanor changes. The hopeful, resourceful friend you've come to know instantly switches to your greatest enemy. "What did my sister ever do to you?" Murp growls.

"Nothing! I like Maddie!"

Murp clenches his big red fist. "You got rid of her because you knew she was the only one who could stop you, then you brought the nest onto the ship to get rid of us too. Didn't you?!"

"No!"

"Wait!" Wumbo raises a hand. He's at the computer terminal now, staring at the code. "I can find the nest."

"How?" Murp asks skeptically.

"This code's not random. It's showing what's happening right now in the game."

"T-minus three minutes," CLIVE chirps.

Wumbo types quickly. "Here's the code for the spiders. By tracing it back, I can . . ."

CLANK!

The ceiling air vent grate hits the ground, and hundreds of deep-space spiders pour into the room.

"WHAT HAPPENED TO THREE MINUTES?!" Princess Palita screams at CLIVE.

You squeeze your eyes closed and wait for it all to be over. You hear the *clickclickclick* of the spiders crawling. You hear the *taptaptap* of Wumbo typing faster. Something crawls on your leg. Then everything goes silent with one final tap.

You slowly reopen your eyes. All the spiders are gone. Wumbo looks exhausted. "What happened?" you ask.

"I deleted the spiders," Wumbo replies.

"You can delete stuff?!" Princess Palita asks. "Is that a normal video game thing?"

"No. I hacked it."

Murp looks sideways at Wumbo. "I thought you were a dentist."

"Oh, right, well . . ." Wumbo looks uncomfortable. Now, you have some questions for the wombat.

SELECT

119 What haven't you been telling us?

121 What else can you hack?

"WOOOOOHOOOOOO!" you yell when you blow up the last vehicle. You're surprised to hear another voice joining your celebration—Princess Palita's.

Ice Maverick cocks his head. "I thought you didn't like video games."

The princess quickly regains her composure. "I like puzzles. That was a puzzle."

"With an explosion at the end."

"Oh, there was an explosion? I didn't notice."

"Palita loves video games, Palita loves video games!" Ice taunts in a singsong voice.

"If you tell a soul, I'm telling everyone about the spiders," Princess Palita fires back. Ice Maverick makes a motion like he's zipping his lips. Palita smiles. "You're not really scared of spiders, are you? You wanted me on weapons because you knew I would like it."

"Guess we'll never know," Ice Maverick replies coyly.

"Well, thanks," Princess Palita says. "Sometimes, I feel like I can't talk to my son because he loves video games, and I can't stand them."

"You have plenty to talk about now," Ice says.

Princess Palita sighs. "Did you know the hologram book was actually addressed to him? The only reason I picked it up was so I could learn enough about video games to talk to him in a way he'd understand."

"That wouldn't have worked," Ice says. "There's nothing worse than an old person trying to relate to kids by memorizing slang."

Palita rolls her eyes. "Thanks for the parenting tip."

"Seriously, it's not that hard. Your son just wants you. Even when he says he doesn't."

Princess Palita gives Ice Maverick a funny look. "Thanks for the parenting tip," she says again, but this time, she means it.

Ice pulls the tank next to the *Starship Crusader*. The dune buggy team arrives at the same time with the power orb. "You guys go ahead," Ice says. "I've got to grab something."

When you hop out of the tank, the earth rumbles.

TURN TO

P. 102

B ❗ ACHIEVEMENT UNLOCKED
PALITA LOVES VIDEO GAMES

CLIVE HELPS YOU up the cliff and leads you to your sleeping quarters. "Wrong room," you say immediately upon walking through the door.

"No, it's not." Princess Palita points to the door placard. There's your name and picture alongside the name "Professor Glugg" and a picture of a blubbery slug wearing reading glasses.

You shake your head. The room you remember had been trashed. This one is spotless. The beds are made. It doesn't smell like old Cheez Whiz. The only thing out of place is a set of starship pajamas on Glugg's bed. You step closer to get a better look at the pajamas and suddenly feel sick. Those are definitely Glugg's pajamas. They're slug-shaped. His name is on his chest. And right next to that name is a perfect blaster hole, complete with burnt edges.

"You blasted him . . ." Wumbo whispers. "You blasted Glugg the Slug."

"This wasn't here before!" you yelp. "It's all different!"

"You're saying you were set up?" Ice Maverick asks.

"Yes!"

"Just like you were set up when you killed Steamroller?" Ice shakes his head. "Lock him up, CLIVE."

How do you get out of this?

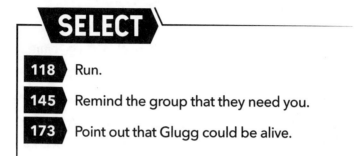

SELECT

118 Run.

145 Remind the group that they need you.

173 Point out that Glugg could be alive.

MURP IS CONFIDENT that he can find his way off the ship in the dark, so he leaves CLIVE with Princess Palita and drops Wumbo into his pocket. You navigate to the airlock by feel, then Murp groans. "I just realized it won't open without electricity."

"Ice Maverick found a secret panel last time we came this way," Wumbo squeaks from Murp's pocket. "Try banging the wall on your left."

Murp hits the wall, and sure enough, a secret passage opens. Your group drops to the floor of the megaship. After finding a safe spot underneath the *Starship Crusader*, you peek at your new surroundings.

This looks nothing like a spaceship. Instead, it appears that you've been transported to a grungy, old factory, complete with tattered conveyor belts and rusty chains. The only clue that you're still in space comes from the factory workers. They're all creatures that could be best described as "muscle frogs."

"It stinks like a swamp in here," Wumbo complains.

"How can you smell?" Murp asks. "You don't have a nose."

"I'm a talking apple, but smell was the unrealistic part for you?" Wumbo asks.

CREEEAAAAK!

Oh no! Your ship's on a conveyor belt, and it's moving! "Where are we going?!" you ask.

Murp holds Wumbo out like a periscope. "Eeeps!" the apple squeaks. "It's a trash compactor!"

You've got to move, but where? The muscle frogs are everywhere. Murp and Wumbo come up with ideas at the same time.

"I need a paper clip," Murp says.

"Either of you good at baseball?" Wumbo asks.

SELECT

20 Go with Murp's solution.

152 Go with Wumbo's solution.

"IT'S ICE MAVERICK," you say.

"WHAT?!"

You were expecting this outburst, so you hold up a hand. "Let me finish."

Ice Maverick does not let you finish. Instead, he grabs your throat and holds you in the air. "What did you say, lizard?"

It's pretty hard to talk with your throat being squeezed, so you let Ice finish.

"Who saved us from the pirates? Who won that dogfight? Who took on an army of space spiders all by himself?"

"You technically brought the spiders on board in the first place," Murp points out.

Ice Maverick fires a blast in Murp's direction without shifting his focus from you. "I don't like you, I don't like your hair, and I especially don't like that you've made me lose a million dollars by getting this wrong." Ice marches to the edge of the arena and throws you.

"CLIVE!" you yell, holding your hand out for rescue.

For the first time all game, CLIVE doesn't move his hand.

E ❶ ACHIEVEMENT UNLOCKED
FINISHED

RETURN TO CHECKPOINT ON P. 59

"STEAMROLLER, YOU'RE UP."

"YES!" Steamroller pumps his fist.

"NO!" The princess jumps in front of you and crosses her arms. Her tarp crinkles. "I forbid it."

"He gives us the best chance because he's the only one who plays video games."

"I'm so good at them," Steamroller says, bouncing in place.

Princess Palita looks like she wants to argue but then glances over her shoulder at the asteroids and steps away. Steamroller leaps into the seat and rubs his hands together. "Watch me, watch me! Here we . . ." Before he gets to "go," he mashes a button, and the ship takes off. You instantly regret handing the controls over to a six-year-old.

"AHHHHH!" Princess Palita and Captain Carter hold each other while Steamroller barrels toward an asteroid. At the last second, the big monster yanks the control wheel and skims the top of the big rock. Then, he dips under another and turns the spaceship sideways to avoid a third. He bobs and weaves through the asteroid field like he's been flying spaceships all of his life—which, if you think about it, he pretty much has.

When the ship clears the final asteroid, Steamroller celebrates with a complicated dance that looks like it was inspired by a video game. "WHO'S YOUR DADDY?!" he yells at no one in particular.

Princess Palita is doing her best to look unimpressed. "You're no one's daddy. You're a child who plays too many video games, and I'm upset that you're being rewarded for it."

Tap-tap-tap.

You look up to see Murp's face behind a vent. He points to CLIVE, then points up. CLIVE telescopes his hand to the ceiling and unscrews the vent.

"Get up here! Now!" Murp yells.

You, Princess Palita, and Captain Carter all hold on to CLIVE, who lifts you through the vent. You join Murp, Wumbo, Ice Maverick, and Maddie inside the duct. That's the whole crew except Steamroller. No way the monster's nine-foot frame is fitting up here.

TURN TO

P.34

H ❗ ACHIEVEMENT UNLOCKED
WHO'S YOUR DADDY?

YOU SLOWLY RAISE your hand. "It's me."

"Finally!" Murp exclaims.

"I don't understand how you did the phone bomb thing," Princess Palita says. "I thought for sure that was Murp."

You shrug. "I don't understand either."

"But you just said that you're the one who did it," the princess says in that slow voice people use when they're talking to a crazy person.

"Because all the evidence says it was me. I shot Steamroller. Professor Glugg was my roommate. I don't remember doing it, but I must have. It's the only thing that makes sense."

"Know what doesn't make sense?" Ice Maverick asks. "You using our one guess on yourself when you're the only one who knows you didn't do it."

"Hahahaha." Someone chuckles an evil chuckle behind you. You turn to see who it could be, but an asteroid smashes your team before you get a chance.

R ❶ ACHIEVEMENT UNLOCKED
NOTHING MAKES SENSE
RETURN TO CHECKPOINT ON P. 59

"THE VENTS!" you yell.

No one understands what you're trying to say.

"They're coming through the vents!"

Everyone except Ice Maverick scrambles to aim at the ceiling vents. "Are you nuts?!" Ice asks.

Clomp. Clomp. Clomp.

Princess Palita pushes Ice Maverick toward a vent. "Help us!"

Clomp. Clomp. Clomp.

Ice Maverick tries spinning around the princess to aim at the door. "Nobody's coming through the vents!"

Just then, the source of the clomping barges through the door. It's Steamroller. "They're coming," he says, before collapsing from exhaustion.

Dozens of space pirates pour into the room behind Steamroller.

E ❗ ACHIEVEMENT UNLOCKED
CLOMP
RETURN TO CHECKPOINT ON P. 34

"I'M A DOCTOR!" you blurt.

"Uh, yeah. We know," Ice Maverick says.

"You don't want to lock up the doctor! What if something bad happens? You need me to heal you."

Ice takes a health pack out of your lab coat pocket. "Guess I'm the doctor now."

You turn to Wumbo for help, but the wombat turns away.

"Lock him up, CLIVE," Ice says.

CLIVE cuffs your hands behind your back while Wumbo and Princess Palita shuffle out of the room. Ice Maverick waits until they leave, then leans close. "I don't really think you did it," he whispers.

"What?! Why didn't you say something?"

"Because I'm about to do something."

"What does that mean?!"

Ice chuckles and slaps your back. CLIVE takes that as a signal to march you into the hallway.

TURN TO

P. 130

ACHIEVEMENT UNLOCKED
I'M THE DOCTOR NOW

"THAT'S NOT ICE MAVERICK!" you blurt.

Murp folds his arms across his chest. "Really?"

"Would the real Ice pass up an opportunity to brag about saving everyone?"

Wumbo squints at the screen. "The computer says it's him."

"He's not talking!" you continue. "All Ice does is talk. Maybe the spiders changed him or something. Like, if we take off the helmet, we'll probably find a big spider inside."

The princess considers this for a moment, then points at CLIVE. "Handcuff Ice."

You breathe a sigh of relief as CLIVE cuffs the soldier. "Thank you."

But Princess Palita's not ready to let you off the hook. "Cuff him too."

"Me?!" You retreat. "Wait! No!" Too late. CLIVE cuffs you too.

"I don't know what to believe, and I'm not taking chances," the princess says.

"Heads up," Wumbo says. "We're back." The loading bar on the wall hits 100 percent, and the world reappears around you pixel by pixel. Your team finds itself surrounded by spiky ice aliens in a frozen cavern. The crew tries fighting back, but it's hopeless with your best warrior in handcuffs. The battle's over before it begins.

⊙ ACHIEVEMENT UNLOCKED
SPIDER GUY
RETURN TO CHECKPOINT ON P. 80

YOU TURN TO ICE MAVERICK. "The rocks are cracked. Why don't you use your pickax?"

"Not gonna work."

"Then you lead us down that other path."

"Wumbo wants to do it."

You take a deep breath to gather your courage. "You told us to stay behind you to stay safe. Now, you want Wumbo to lead. What's going on?"

"What are you trying to say?" Ice Maverick puts his hand on his blaster.

When Ice reaches for his weapon, Wumbo snatches the soldier's pickax and tosses it to you. You swing at the boulder, which crumbles like it's made of granola. You glare at Ice, who shrugs back.

"I don't know why this would be surprising to you," Ice says. "I told you before that I want the prize for myself. And now I'll tell you something else: I don't change."

"You're going to need us," Wumbo says. "Just wait."

Ice chuckles. "I know you were trying to look tough right there, but it's hard to take you seriously with that furry, little face."

Wumbo huffs and clenches his fists in a way that, you have to admit, looks adorable. You use the pickax to clear the rest of the boulders, Ice blasts a few enemies, and you finally climb out of the canyon. When you reach the top, you can barely open your eyes. It's so bright!

"Hot, hot, hot!" Wumbo yelps and jumps on one foot.

As a cold-blooded reptile, you don't mind the heat. You pick up Wumbo to get his feet off the sand, wait for your eyes to adjust to the brightness, then look at your ship. Your heart sinks. A truck-sized asteroid is sticking out of the *Starship Crusader*'s roof. You can't begin to imagine how you'd clear it. You turn to Ice Maverick for help, but someone's standing between you and Ice. It's a giant made of clay.

"Welcome to Planet Groob," the giant says. Then, he knocks you out with a club.

TURN TO

P.72

D ❶ ACHIEVEMENT UNLOCKED
PLANET GROOB

THUD!

The ship shakes. Uh-oh. You realize that nobody's steering the ship now that Steamroller's dead.

BOOM!

Something smacks into the ship so hard that it starts tumbling.

"*Starship Crusader* has been struck by a Category 7 asteroid," CLIVE calmly explains. "Thrusters three and four have sustained critical damage."

"Everyone to the bridge!" Ice commands.

The crew stumbles back to the bridge, then Ice straps himself to the captain's chair and does his best to steer the damaged ship. All he really manages to do is spin it some more and make you feel sick.

"Let someone else drive, Blaster Boy!" the princess yells.

"I've got it!" Ice Maverick fires back.

You'd love to trust that he has everything under control, but one glimpse out the window tells you that things are not only spinning out of control but also spinning directly toward a rust-red planet. Ice Maverick leans forward and grips the controls like he actually believes that he has some say in what the ship does. You spiral faster. Everyone screams. The ship enters the planet's atmosphere. You can now pinpoint the mountain range that you're going to crash into.

At the last second, Ice Maverick pulls back on the controls as hard as he can. It's certainly not enough to stop the crash, but it levels out the ship just enough for it to bounce—"OUCH!"—then tumble—"AHH!"—then wedge itself into a canyon. "Ooooooooooof."

Smoke fills the bridge, and an alarm sounds. Ice Maverick raises a fist in victory. "Nailed it."

"You destroyed the ship!" Wumbo squeaks.

"Relax, it's a video game. That was going to happen no matter what we did." Ice Maverick shuts up the alarm by shooting it, then he casually jumps out of his seat. "Woodchuck, let's explore this planet. Everyone else, help Murp fix the ship."

> *Which group would you like to join? Use this opportunity to learn more about your fellow crewmates.*

SELECT

76 Wumbo and Ice Maverick.

18 Murp, Maddie, and Princess Palita.

YOU STUDY YOUR BLASTER. It looks way more complicated than it needs to be. Is there a switch you accidentally flipped from "stun" to "kill"? Doesn't seem to be. After turning it over a few times, you hold it in your right hand and pick up Wumbo's blaster with your left. You compare the two weapons. Notice any differences?

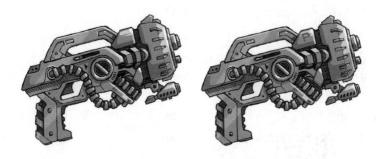

> *Now, it's time to investigate Captain Carter's demise.*
> *Again, choose only one of the options below.*

SELECT

87	Investigate the bomb.
44	Question Wumbo.
100	Question Princess Palita.

L ❗ ACHIEVEMENT UNLOCKED
STUN/KILL

"CHECK OUT THAT BUTTON," Wumbo says. "That's got to be an emergency shutoff." You spot a big red button on the wall that's glowing invitingly. "Throw me at the button, then grab their weapons while they're distracted."

Murp nods. "Doc, you throw. I'll get the weapons." Before you can protest, Murp crawls behind a pillar.

"I can't hit that!" you tell Wumbo.

"You got it! I believe in you!"

With that pep talk from an apple, you pick up Wumbo, concentrate on the button, then deliver your best fastball. You miss, and not just by a few inches. You actually hit an alien standing 10 feet away from the button.

"ROWWW—" The alien gets vaporized before it can draw its blaster. Murp must have found a weapon after all! He pops out of hiding, stops the conveyor belt by shooting the emergency shutoff, then screams, "RUN!"

All the aliens start shooting at Murp, who's now retreating and using scrap metal as a shield. You pick up Wumbo and sprint down a hallway to join Murp. Fortunately, speed doesn't seem to be this alien race's thing. You run and run, then bump into Princess Palita and CLIVE. "How did you get here?!" everyone screams at once.

TURN TO

P. 82

T ❗ ACHIEVEMENT UNLOCKED
TERRIBLE AT BASEBALL

YOUR CREW SQUEEZES each other tightly. The ground starts trembling, then shaking, then violently bucking. It gets so bad that you have to close your eyes to concentrate on your grip. Finally, the shaking stops. You look around and find that the earthquake didn't just go away—the ground itself disappeared. Your group is floating through a long, dark cave. The only light is coming from the glow of Wumbo's laptop screen.

"Heads up, everyone," Wumbo says. "I had to adjust the fast-forward code from skip to scrub to keep the system stable."

"Does it count as a heads-up if we didn't understand one word you said?" Princess Palita asks.

"Instead of skipping from level to level, we now have to survive a sped-up version of the game," Wumbo says.

"How sped-up?"

The princess gets her answer when a glowing eel alien bursts out of the wall and zaps her before she can scream. You toss over a health pack right before a dozen more eels emerge. For the next minute—the longest minute of your life—your crew bounces off of walls in zero gravity to dodge lightning bolts fired at triple-speed. You use four more health packs to get everyone through the gauntlet.

Next up: City of Smashy Bots. Each crewmember gets a mech suit to deal with unreasonably upset robots destroying a city at warp speed. You spend the level dodging supercharged punches and crumbling buildings while tossing health packs to your team.

The next level is an intergalactic dogfight, which gives everyone a break except for Ice Maverick. He has to pilot the ship and fire at enemy spacecraft at the same time. You'd like to help, but the game is sped up so much that you feel like you're on that carnival ride that sticks you to the wall by spinning fast. You use the break to glance into your lab coat pocket. Only six health packs left. You used twice that many on the robot level.

Your next destination is an erupting volcano with magma monsters. You use three health packs on that level.

Next up: Prehistoric Planet. Two more health packs.

Finally, there's a haunted space station where you're forced to use your last health pack. "I'm out," you say just as Ice Maverick defeats the final galactic ghost.

The game starts glitching again. The next level goes through several cycles of trying and failing to load.

"I'm hot," Murp complains. "Is anyone else hot?" You realize that the temperature hasn't cooled since the volcano planet.

"The system's overloaded again," Wumbo says. "It doesn't have enough memory left to run the next level. I might be able to scale things back to get this running, but it won't be pretty."

"Do it!" Ice Maverick yells.

Wumbo types something, then *BLOOOOP*—everything gets real blocky, like an arcade game from the '80s. An army of pixelated blobs descends from above. It's just like that *Space Invaders* game you remember seeing one time on TV. Did Wumbo take you back in time?

"What's happening?!" you yell. Or at least, you try to yell. You can't talk because nobody talked in those old games—there wasn't enough memory. Plus, you're a jumble of pixels like everything else, and you're not sure whether you even have a mouth.

The alien army starts shooting white dots that are probably supposed to be lasers, so your crew takes cover and returns fire. Only one member of your crew is landing any shots. That's got to be Ice Maverick. After a while, however, you notice that not even the Ice Maverick blob can get any shots off. While most of the aliens are firing randomly, one enemy seems to be strategically placing lasers to keep your team pinned.

The *BLOOP*s are getting closer. Your team is hopelessly trapped.

Wait a second. There should be five people trapped behind this rock with you. Instead, there's only four. The traitor's out there with the aliens!

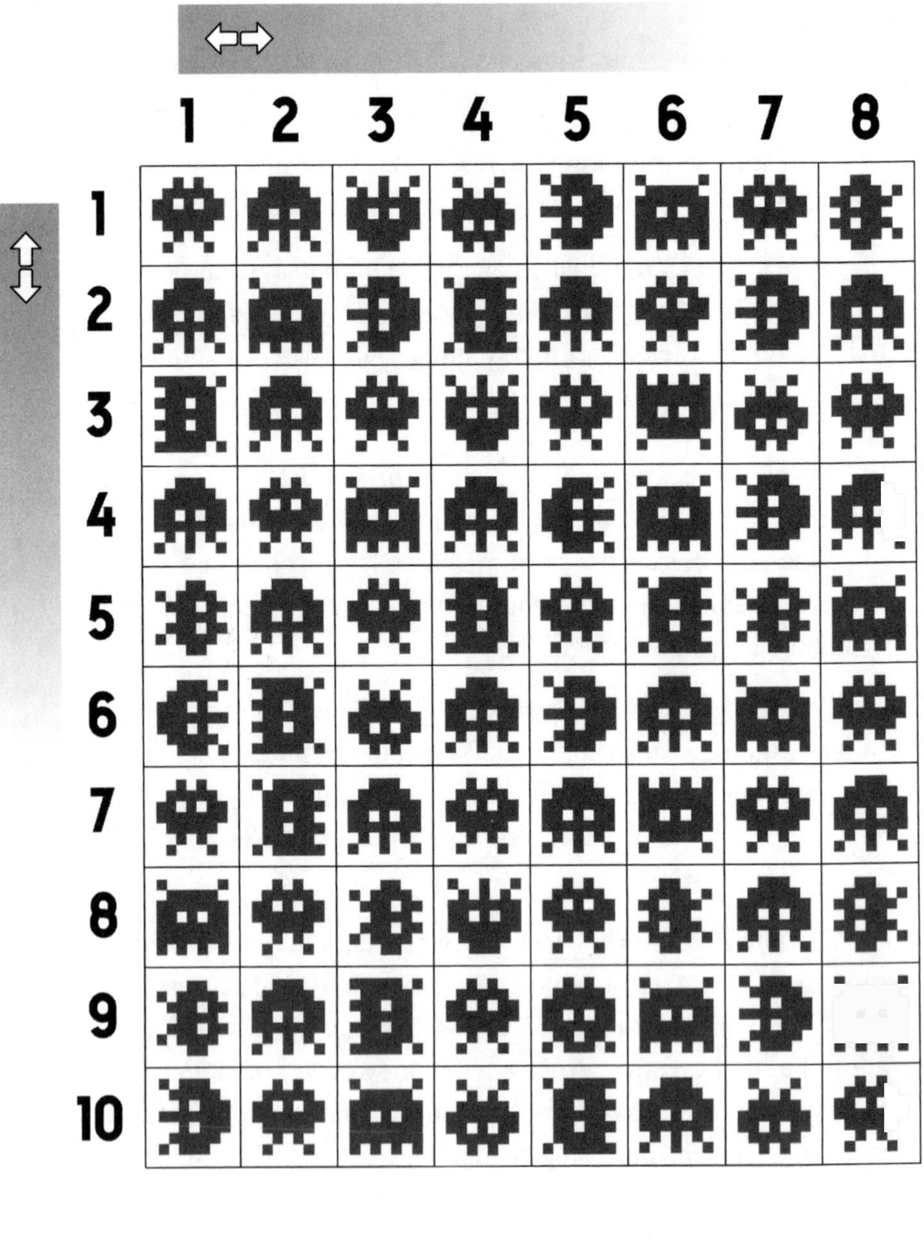

This level features three types of aliens, all turned different directions. However, if you look closely, you'll find one alien that doesn't match any of the others. That's your traitor. Turn to that alien's coordinates to reach the next section.

9 10 11 12 13 14 15 16

TURN TO P. ___ ___

⟺ ⇕

BY THE TIME YOU ASSEMBLE Murp's Slug-O-Matic, Ice Maverick has destroyed most of the caravan with his tank. "Gun it!" Murp shouts to Maddie. She pulls next to the power orb vehicle. It looks like a military moving truck, except the back is tattered so you can see the orb glowing inside. The driver snarls at your crew. You wave, then angle the Slug-O-Matic his way.

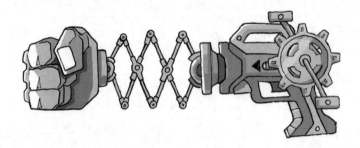

"Now!" Murp yells.

You squeeze the Slug-O-Matic trigger. Unfortunately, you underestimated the force of its kickback. You not only miss the driver but also nearly fall out of your own vehicle. When you get back up, you see that several more bad guys have emerged.

"Doc, you aim!" Murp says. "Wumbo, fire!"

You doubt this will work, but the Slug-O-Matic turns out to be the perfect weapon against the clay monsters. They may be big and scary, but they don't have nearly the reach of Murp's creation. By working together, you and Wumbo clear the entire truck. You punch the driver last, which causes the truck to drift toward the edge of a cliff.

"CLIVE!" Murp yells while pointing at the enemy truck. The robot extends his arms to create a bridge. Your whole team scrambles across, and Murp takes the wheel.

"That was AWESOME!" you celebrate.

"The Slug-O-Matic was genius!" Wumbo says. "You came up with that on the spot?!"

Murp grins at Maddie. "I don't remember; have I ever built a Slug-O-Matic before?"

Maddie rolls her eyes. "Yes, he's built that dumb thing out of Legos and rubber bands so many times. It's his worst invention."

"You're an inventor in real life?!" you ask.

Murp wiggles his eyebrows.

"He's not an inventor!" Maddie says. "He's a sixth grader who likes building things that annoy his sister."

"That's the definition of an inventor," Murp says as he parks the truck next to the *Starship Crusader*.

Ice Maverick and Princess Palita pull up in their tank at the same time. Then, the ground starts shaking.

TURN TO

P. 102

H ❶ ACHIEVEMENT UNLOCKED
SLUG-O-MATIC

YOU CRAWL TOWARD WUMBO. Ice Maverick points his blaster at you as a warning, but you raise a hand. "I can prove who the traitor is. Please. Give me a chance."

When you reach Wumbo, you pull a grenade from his chest strap. You stand shakily to your feet, then use the last of your strength to heave the grenade at CLIVE.

"AHHHH!" everyone screams and ducks. But CLIVE doesn't let the grenade explode. Instead, he telescopes his arm and picks it out of the air.

You cock your head at the robot. "Why did you catch it? I didn't point." CLIVE doesn't respond, but his usual cheesy grin falters for just a second. You turn to the group. "We all thought CLIVE was an NPC—that he was part of the game. He's not." You point a finger at CLIVE. "That's Professor Glugg."

CLIVE looks at the grenade in his hand, then back at you. His eyes are full of hatred now. He grits his teeth, then whips the grenade at you. You stand tall and let it bounce harmlessly off your chest.

You nod at Wumbo. "Fake grenades in the front."

"Always."

"I don't understand," Princess Palita says.

"That's because you don't play video games," you reply. "In video games, NPCs that follow you around might be annoying, but at least they're always right. CLIVE was never right. Remember when he said we'd beaten that big Urg monster when we hadn't? Or when he got the spider countdown wrong?"

"He got the name of the three-sun planet wrong," Ice Maverick realizes.

"The name of this planet too!" Princess Palita adds.

"Think about it," you say. "CLIVE never told us anything we couldn't see for ourselves. He was always making it up as he went along."

Wumbo's computer dings. He leans closer, then his eyes widen. "It's the three clues the game gave us: the letters *N-P-C*." He looks up. "Doc's right."

"It's always the butler," Princess Palita says with disgust.

Clap. Clap. Clap. Clap.

The Pemberton hologram is back, and it's slow-clapping. "Congratulations. You've cracked the case. At this time, the traitor will be removed from the game." Pieces of CLIVE's robot body start turning digital and streaming into the sky, revealing a slug underneath. This version of Professor Glugg is way uglier than the photo you'd seen earlier. He's covered with brown warts and a thick layer of slime.

"Well done," Pemberton continues. "I'd like to use this final recording to—"

SMASH!

CLIVE telescopes a fist straight through Wumbo's computer, freezing both the hologram message and the removal process. He turns to you and sneers. With part of his CLIVE face stripped away, the half-robot, half-slug creature looks especially terrifying. He grabs your neck. "Think you're pretty smart, huh, lizard?" CLIVE gurgles. "You don't know the half of it. I've worked too hard to lose this money."

"Too late for that," Ice Maverick says.

CLIVE shoots a fist across the arena to punch Ice in the chest. The punch is so strong that it cracks Ice's armor and drops the soldier to the ground. "It's not too late because Hacker Boy can reprogram the game to send me the money," CLIVE says.

"I can't reprogram anything!" Wumbo squeaks. "You broke my computer, and you probably broke the game too!"

CLIVE extends his arm to dangle you over the edge of the arena. "You'd better try if you want to save the good doctor." CLIVE's eyes look crazy. He could drop you at any moment.

Princess Palita tries buying you more time. "How did you do it?"

CLIVE cracks an evil grin. He's clearly proud of his work and all too happy to monologue. "A note was waiting for me when I entered the game: eliminate the crew one by one to win a million dollars. I knew I had to act fast if I was going to pull it off. Just one problem—I'd entered the game as a fat, slow slug. Then I saw my roommate and realized I had a chance. A lizard! I could buy myself all the time I needed by cranking up the air conditioner and making the cold-blooded reptile sleep. So I knocked him out, then spied on everyone from the vents."

"That's why they were slimy," Princess Palita says. "Gross."

"My big break came when I found the computer room. I'm a bit of a programmer myself, you know."

Wumbo stops working on the laptop and gasps. "Spritexfr wasn't a trap! It was in the computer's history because you'd used the program on yourself."

"You all don't give him enough credit," CLIVE says. "I think he's the smartest of the bunch. You're right, woodchuck. I lured the butler robot into the computer room, then used the program to trade my slug body for his. After that, it was all easy. I set up a snoring dummy on my bed to make Doc look crazy.

I swapped Steamroller's uniform with a paper one. I built two phone bombs—one for the captain and one to frame Murp. Then, I broke the magnetic system to lock everyone in their rooms and turned off the air conditioner to wake up Doc."

"You really thought of everything," Murp says with fake admiration.

"Except for the EMP," CLIVE says. "I should have played dead when that ship took out our electricity. Fortunately, none of you dummies noticed."

CLIVE's story makes so many things add up, but something's still bugging you. "Why didn't you finish me off when you had a chance during the *Space Invaders* thing?"

"Are you kidding? You set me up beautifully! When Ice shot me, I thought I was done. Everyone would see the damage and realize I was the traitor. Of course, I could fix myself, but that would look suspicious since all the health packs were gone. By keeping you alive and hurt, I could repair myself in the dark and give everyone rock-solid evidence that you were the traitor."

"Too bad it didn't work," you say, unable to resist the jab.

That jab turns out to be super not worth it. CLIVE scowls, then throws you to the ground. He lifts his smelly slug foot over your head. "Bye, Doc. I hated being your roommate."

CRUNCH!

CLIVE's stomp makes a sickening sound. You realize after a few moments that the sound wasn't your skull. Instead, Ice Maverick dove in at the last second, and CLIVE's stomp shattered the soldier's armor. Ice rolls in pain next to you.

"Fine, I'll finish you both," CLIVE says. He lifts his foot to stomp again. When he does, you notice something weird. The foot is smaller than before. CLIVE notices it too. He stares at the foot, then recoils when he sees it stream into the air, pixel by pixel. He spins to find Wumbo. "STOP!" he bellows as he rumbles toward the wombat.

Murp and Princess Palita are standing guard in front of the computer with their fists raised. Of course, they're no match for the robot slug, but they'll do whatever they can to protect their friend.

"Almost done!" yells Wumbo.

CLIVE makes one final effort to dive onto Wumbo's computer, but the last of his body disappears midair.

As soon as CLIVE's gone, Murp and Princess Palita run to check on you and Ice Maverick. "Are you two OK?" the princess asks.

"No," you both groan.

"We need a health pack!" Murp yells. "Wumbo, make that happen!"

"A little busy trying to keep the game from falling apart!" Wumbo responds.

Ice Maverick pulls out a health pack with a shaky hand. "I've got one."

"Nice! Now, we need one more for Doc!"

But instead of using the health pack on himself, Ice surprises everyone by tossing it to you.

"I can't," you say. "You saved me."

Ice waves you off. "You saved us all. Plus, I stole it from you in the first place."

The edges of the arena start crumbling. "What's going on, Wumbo?" Murp asks.

"I'm getting us home!"

A swirling blue portal appears across the arena. "That's Ice's!" Wumbo yells. "Get him there, now!"

You use the health pack, then help Murp and Princess Palita drag the battered soldier to his portal. "That was pretty heroic," you say. "I'm going to tell everyone I met the real-life Batman."

"Save it, lizard," Ice growls. With that, you roll him into the portal.

"Murp's next!" Wumbo says when another portal appears.

"Say hi to Maddie for us!" Princess Palita yells as Murp jumps in.

At this point, the arena is really falling apart. The princess has to jump onto your shoulders just before a block crumbles under her feet. Finally, Wumbo hits ENTER. The final three portals appear at once. Wumbo points to the portals. "Me, Princess, Doc."

"Nice job!" the princess says.

Wumbo allows himself a smile. "No biggie," he says before diving into his portal.

You step toward your portal, but the princess stops you. "I have a better idea," she says. What do you do?

SELECT

176 Follow the princess.

96 Go home.

WAIT. THE PIRATES' FOOTSTEPS land with thuds, not clomps. You suddenly recognize the sound in the hallway, and you realize that the crew is about to make a huge mistake. "Don't shoot!" you yell, jumping in front of the door. "It's Steamroller!"

The words are barely out of your mouth when Steamroller barrels into you. "They're coming!"

"Suit up!" Ice Maverick points to the last remaining suit. Steamroller zips it just as the first pirate enters the armory. This wave of pirates is twice as ferocious as the first. The entire crew has to work together to fend off the invasion—Ice and Maddie can't handle it by themselves this time. You quickly grow winded from trying to keep up with the mayhem. When the last pirate goes down, you put your hands on your knees and gasp for air.

You feel a presence behind you. You look up. Steamroller is pointing over your shoulder with wide eyes. You don't need to turn around to understand that you're about to get sliced. You pull an Ice Maverick by diving forward and shooting Steamroller.

POOF!

Your plasma blast doesn't bounce off of Steamroller's uniform and into the pirate like you expected. Instead, it vaporizes Steamroller.

Ice Maverick takes care of the pirate. Everyone stares at the spot where Steamroller was standing, then turns to gawk at you. "What did you do?" Maddie finally whispers.

"I didn't—well, I did, but I thought that—I mean, you saw how . . ." you stammer.

CLIVE clears his throat. "It is my duty to reveal this message when the first crewmember gets eliminated."

"FIRST crewmember?!" everyone shrieks.

CLIVE holds out his hand, and a hologram appears. It's James Desmond Pemberton, the rich guy you met in the first hologram. He looks quite pleased with himself. "Hello! Hope you're enjoying the game! Please don't mourn your fallen crewmember. Your friend is fine! This is a video game, after all. Everyone knows video game deaths aren't real. Seriously, it's no biggie. Your friend is back at home, likely a little confused, but very OK. I'm guessing you're also a bit confused."

Everyone is indeed confused.

"Let me tell you what's going on." The guy wiggles his eyebrows to build suspense. "Aren't mystery stories great?"

Princess Palita nods vigorously. Everyone else looks more confused than ever.

"I love mysteries, and I love video games," Pemberton continues. "The problem is that both are so predictable. That's why you're here. I've been given the opportunity to use old Bionosoft technology to create a mystery where even I don't know what happens. Here's how it works: I've reprogrammed the game to assign one of you the role of traitor. I don't know who got that role. CLIVE doesn't know who got that role. The only one who knows is the traitor. The traitor's job is to eliminate the rest of the crew one by one without being discovered."

You take an uneasy step back from the rest of your crew.

"Traitor, if you're the last one standing, you win one million dollars. Everyone else, it's your job to survive until the end of the game, where you'll get a chance to solve the mystery. Beat the game, unmask the traitor, and you win the million dollars." Pemberton pauses to let that sink in. He has the world's biggest grin on his face. "Any questions?"

Everyone shouts questions at once.

"Too bad," Pemberton interrupts. "I'm not giving answers. Now, go play the game. I'm paying a lot of money for you to entertain me. Go, go, go!" With that, Pemberton's hologram disappears.

As soon as the hologram disappears, Captain Carter points at you. "It's the lizard."

The group turns on you.

"What's wrong with you?"

"He was just a kid!"

"TRAITOR!"

Princess Palita raises her hand to stop the madness. Nobody pays attention, so she sticks two fingers in her mouth and does that loud whistle that only moms know how to do. That silences the group.

"I may not know about video games, but I've been preparing my whole life to be in a mystery," the princess says. "I read a mystery novel a week. I can quote every episode of *Murder, She Wrote*. I even sat through those awful Sherlock Holmes movies where he punches people instead of solves mysteries. I don't know which one of you is the traitor yet, but I'll tell you this: the lizard doctor was framed."

"You're the traitor!" Captain Carter shouts, sticking to her proven strategy of wildly throwing accusations.

"It's not me, sweetie," the princess replies calmly.

"Oh yeah?!" The captain steps toward the princess, eager to take the upper hand. "Your bracelet thingy opened the door! You're literally the only person who could come in and switch his uniform!"

"First of all, if I were the traitor, you'd be gone already because you annoy me the most."

Captain Carter huffs.

"Second, why don't you take a look at this and let me know what you see?" The princess picks up one of the fallen ceiling grates.

"I dunno," the captain mumbles.

The princess turns to Ice Maverick. "How about you, Blaster Boy? Notice anything?"

Ice Maverick throws his hands in the air, as if to ask what he did to get involved in this.

"I'll give you a hint." Princess Palita grabs another grate. This one is all mangled. "See it now? This one looks like it was bashed in by a space pirate. The first one wasn't bent at all. Why is that? Because someone already broke in here by unscrewing the grate."

The princess tosses the grate to Ice Maverick, who lets it bounce off of his body. "You're in a mystery. If you want to live, you'll listen to me," she says, throwing the soldier's words from earlier back at him. "The traitor has almost certainly set another booby trap. It'll be something that gets used all the time. Be careful. Next—"

Ding!

Captain Carter stops listening and pulls out her glowing rectangle.

Oh no! You realize immediately that the glowing rectangle isn't some harmless prank. It's a bomb. "DROP THAT!"

Captain Carter sticks out her tongue in defiance. That's the last thing she gets to do in the game.

BOOM!

Now, the two crewmembers are gone. Princess Palita looks like she knows she should be sad about Captain Carter's demise, but she can't keep the giddy smile off of her face. "Well gang, we've got a crime scene to investigate. Everyone, start looking for clues. Nobody leaves this room. Most of all, remember that the traitor is right here. Don't trust anyone."

First, investigate what happened to Steamroller.
Choose wisely—you have time for only one option.

SELECT

151 Examine the blaster.

172 Investigate the air vent.

41 Look closer at the uniform.

YOU USE YOUR STICKY LIZARD HANDS to climb to the ceiling. Had the grate actually been unscrewed like Princess Palita claimed? When you reach the vent, you discover that not only was the princess right but also the traitor had actually left behind evidence.

"CLIVE!" you yell loud enough for the entire crew to hear. You want to make sure that everyone sees that you didn't hide this evidence yourself. When you have the robot's attention, you point at the vent. CLIVE's eyes turn green, he snakes his arm deep into the vent, then he pulls out an oversized, rumpled jumpsuit. It's Steamroller's original uniform! There's no doubt now that someone sabotaged Steamroller.

> *Now, it's time to investigate Captain Carter's demise.*
> *Again, choose only one of the options below.*

SELECT

87 Investigate the bomb.

44 Question Wumbo.

100 Question Princess Palita.

C ❗ ACHIEVEMENT UNLOCKED
SABOTAGE

"HEAR ME OUT," you say, although you know that no one in the history of the world has been heard out after saying "hear me out." You take a deep breath. "We don't know that Glugg's dead."

Princess Palita shrugs. "OK."

"If he's not dead, then he's got to be playing dead, right? And if he's playing dead, then he's definitely the traitor!"

"He wasn't with us on that planet, so I don't see how he could have killed Maddie," the princess says.

"He's probably working with someone in this room!"

"Yeah. You," Ice Maverick says.

You realize that you're down to your last few seconds of freedom before CLIVE locks you up, so you start tearing through the room to find evidence that you're not crazy. The trash cans are empty. The closet is clean. Then, just as CLIVE produces a pair of handcuffs, you spot something under the bed.

"Aha!" You pull out the canister of hypersleep gas and hoist it proudly above your head. "See?! I wasn't lying!"

Princess Palita grabs the canister from your hands and holds it close to your face. "This look legit to you, Doc?"

Now that you're actually studying the canister, you have to admit that it looks pretty fishy. The word "Hypersleep," for example, is handwritten on a piece of masking tape. The canister itself looks like a rusty scuba tank. Princess Palita unscrews the top to reveal that the only thing it's holding is a bunch of smelly garbage.

"See!" You point at the garbage. "That proves my story!"

"Which story? The one that you couldn't join us for a week because you were in hypersleep?" Princess Palita taps the canister. "Obviously, that wasn't the case." She motions for CLIVE. "Lock him up."

CLIVE cuffs your hands, grabs your arm with a surprisingly strong grip, and marches you down the hallway.

TURN TO

P. 130

❶ ACHIEVEMENT UNLOCKED

RUSTY SCUBA GARBAGE

"IT WAS ICE MAVERICK!" you shout. "He killed Professor Glugg!"

"And how exactly did that happen?" Murp asks.

"Um, well, what if the person we think is Ice Maverick is actually Professor Glugg?"

"So now the professor killed Ice Maverick?" Princess Palita asks.

You hadn't thought of that, but it sounds good so you roll with it. "Yes! Exactly! We haven't seen Ice's face. Who knows what's behind the mask?"

"But Glugg is a slug," Murp points out.

"And slugs are squishy!" you say. "They can squish into any shape."

Ice Maverick flexes a muscle. Even with the thick suit, you notice an impressive bicep bulge. Murp squeezes it. "Doesn't feel squishy to me, Doc."

"Right! That's because space slugs aren't squishy."

"You literally just said they're squishy." Murp narrows his eyes.

"You're squishy!"

ZAP!

Now you're dead.

RETURN TO CHECKPOINT ON P. 80

"WE'RE FOLLOWING WUMBO," Princess Palita says.

"Wait, no! I want to go home!"

Too late. She takes your hand and pulls you into the portal. On the other side, you find yourself holding a woman's hand. She looks kind of like the mom of this kid named Zac from your school. "Mrs. Taylor?" you ask.

"Shhh!" she whispers.

You're standing in the biggest bathroom you've ever seen. It's got a super-high ceiling and a bathtub that looks like it came from a French castle. It even has two toilets! Who could possibly need two toilets in the same bathroom?! Wait, is this Wumbo's house?

The mom (who's definitely Mrs. Taylor—you're sure of it now) creeps into a bedroom that's even fancier than the bathroom. You feel weird sneaking through someone else's house, but Mrs. Taylor sure doesn't. She spots a man lying on the bed with his hand on his forehead. Instead of giving him space like a normal person would, she points and screams, "AHA!"

"AHHHHHHH!" The man's so scared that he tumbles off his bed. When he stands back up, it's your turn to scream. You recognize the face. It's James Desmond Pemberton himself!

"I knew it!" Mrs. Taylor says. "Haha! Gotcha, Wumbo!"

Pemberton sighs. "How long have you known?"

"I knew you had to be a character in the game as soon as you told us about the mystery. If I were paying all that money for a mystery, I'd want to solve it myself, not watch a bunch of strangers bumble around. For a while, I thought it was Doc, but then you hacked the computer and refused to look at the answer key."

"I wanted to figure out the mystery for myself!"

"And I don't blame you! The thing that sealed it, though, was you saying 'no biggie' just like you did in the hologram. Nobody says that anymore."

Pemberton looks at you glumly. "I guess you're Dr. Iz? Great. A kid solved the mystery before me." He sighs, then walks to a computer in the corner of his room. "Oh well, guess I'll try again."

"No!" Mrs. Taylor exclaims.

"Don't worry, I'll send you home and start over with a new group."

Mrs. Taylor jumps in front of the computer. "You can't keep putting people into video games!"

Pemberton looks genuinely confused. "Sure I can. The technology I bought lets me do it as many times as I want."

"Wait," you interject. "I thought you programmed it yourself."

"I programmed the mystery part, but Bionosoft is the only company that figured out how to put people inside video games. I had to buy that part."

"But Bionosoft got shut down."

Pemberton shrugs. "Some guy on the internet sold it to me."

"Who?!"

"I met him on a hacker forum, so I don't know his real name. He calls himself the 'Builder.'"

"You used stolen technology bought from a criminal with a fake name to trap strangers in video games, and you can't see the problem with that?!" Mrs. Taylor asks.

Pemberton waves her off. "It's harmless."

"IT ALMOST KILLED US!"

Pemberton holds up a finger. "But it didn't. And now you have a million dollars, which I think we can all agree is more than enough to make up for whatever minor inconvenience you experienced in there."

"GETTING KILLED IS NOT A MINOR INCONVENIENCE!"

"The money already transferred to your account. Let me show you. It'll make you feel better." Pemberton taps the keyboard a few times, then stiffens. He leans forward and types something else. "No," he says. "Nonononono."

"What's wrong?" Mrs. Taylor asks.

Pemberton looks like he's about to puke. "It's gone."

"The program?"

"MY MONEY! It's all gone!" Pemberton starts typing frantically, then stops when a message appears.

The Builder has your money. It's gone. I don't know what he's planning on doing with it, but it's not good.

I need you to help me investigate by finding every possible ending to complete the game 100 percent. Each ending has a secret letter that you can fill in on the next page. Once you find all the letters, you'll uncover a secret code that you can enter at escapefromavideogame.com. That code will unlock a story that'll tell you everything I've learned about the Builder.

Good luck. And sorry about your money.

❶ ACHIEVEMENT UNLOCKED
VICTORY

Secret Message

Fill in the secret letter that goes with each achievement. When you enter all the letters, you'll spell a phrase. Enter that phrase at escapefromavideogame.com to unlock a secret story.

___ **ROBOT PRETZEL**

___ **UNNECESSARY WATERFALL**

___ **NO EVIDENCE IS THE WORST EVIDENCE**

___ **GOOP, GLOP, GULP**

___ **SOMETHING A PIRATE WOULD SAY**

___ **READY TO RUMBLE**

___ **I'M THE DOCTOR NOW**

___ **STUDENT DRIVER**

___ **THE GHOST**

___ **WHO'S YOUR DADDY?**

___ **AAHOOGA**

___ **POOPY HAIR**

___ **DUMB GUARD**

___ **VICTORY**

___ **STUN/KILL**

___ **PLANET GROOB**

___ **NO OFFENSE**

___ **CLUE-ISH**

___ PALITA LOVES VIDEO GAMES

___ CLOMP

___ IT'S NOT POLITE TO POINT

___ SMART FOR A WOODCHUCK

___ NOTHING MAKES SENSE

___ HEAVY STUFF

___ MACGYVER HACKING

___ FINISHED

___ SABOTAGE

___ YOU'RE SQUISHY

___ THE ASTEROID ALWAYS WINS

___ HALLOWEEN COSTUME

___ HYPERACTIVE SLEEP

___ UNFIXABLE

___ NOT A DENTIST

___ PERRY MASON

___ DUMB TOUPEE LIZARD

___ FIRST INTERROGATION

___ SO SUCKY

___ TERRIBLE AT BASEBALL

___ NEW TAIL SCHOOL

___ SLUG-O-MATIC

___ BLUE SCREEN OF DEATH

___ SPIDER GUY

___ RUSTY SCUBA GARBAGE

___ IT WAS ALL A DREAM

___ TOO CHEESY

___ DYING CLUE

VISIT ESCAPEFROMAVIDEOGAME.COM
TO UNLOCK YOUR ADVENTURE.

NOPE. TOO DANGEROUS. Not enough information.

When you tap "NO," the hologram disappears, and the book transforms into a normal book. Except it's not the book you remember. This book is now *The Cheesemaker's Daughter: Amish Country Lovebirds Book #17,* with a cover that features a woman in a bonnet staring longingly at a barn. You flip through the story. Here's the last page:

"Eliza. Look at me," Amos says.

A single tear runs down Eliza's cheek when she looks into Amos's earthy brown eyes. They are as tender as his arms are rugged.

"I don't care if this sounds cheesy," Amos says. "You melt my heart like mozzarella."

"Oh, Amos!"

He puts his finger on her lips and continues. "Eliza, I'm fondue you. We brie-long together. I don't want to spend my whole life thinking shoulda woulda gouda, so I need to ask you something." He bends down on one knee. "Will you marry me?"

Eliza clutches her heart and starts sobbing. "You cheddar believe it."

❗ ACHIEVEMENT UNLOCKED
TOO CHEESY

RETURN TO CHECKPOINT ON P. 11

Hints and Solutions

P. 16-17

By following the clues around the room, you'll find the numbers "2" and "3" circled on the calendar. Turn to page 23 to reach the next section.

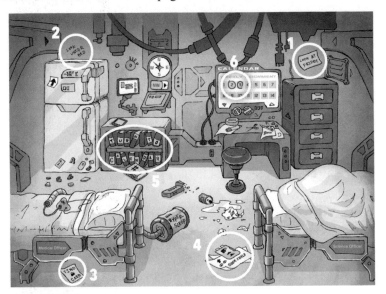

P. 48-49

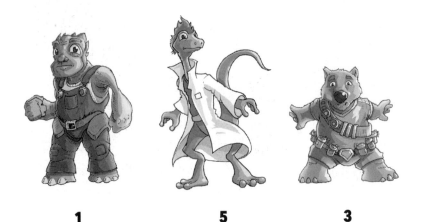

1	**5**	**3**

P. 58

Compare the compasses in the two rooms. What could cause two compasses on the same ship to show different directions? Also, note the magnets sliding off the refrigerator and paper clips standing up by themselves.

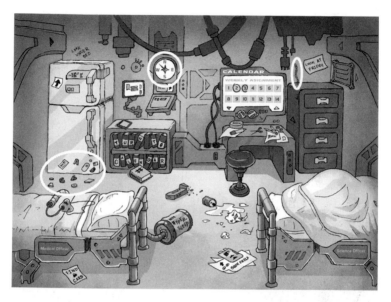

P. 66–67

Match the size of the explosions to the size of the vehicles to find the right combination.

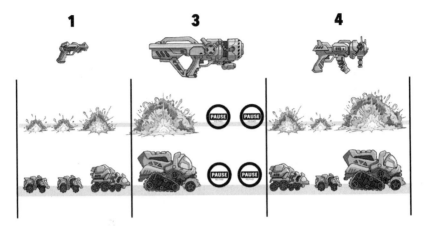

P. 94–95

See the soda bottle in the bottom right corner? A sealed soda bottle will explode if it freezes.

P. 128-129

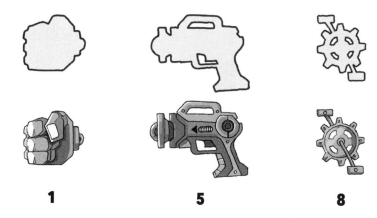

1   **5**   **8**

P. 151

Notice the small *P* engraved on your blaster. What could it mean?

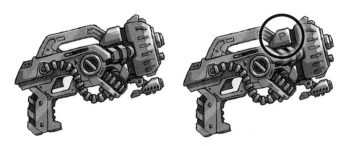

P. 156-157